TWO LINES

Two Lines Press

TWO LINES   WORLD WRITING IN TRANSLATION
XXIV, SPRING 2016

Two Lines Press

Editor
CJ Evans
Senior Editors
Scott Esposito
Michael Holtmann
Production Editor
Jessica Sevey
Associate Editor
Marthine Satris
Founding Editor
Olivia Sears
Design
Ragina Johnson
Cover Design
Quemadura

TWO LINES
Issue 24
ISBN 978-1-931883-52-8
ISSN 1525-5204

© 2016 by Two Lines Press
582 Market Street, Suite 700
San Francisco, CA 94104
www.twolinespress.com
twolines@catranslation.org

Two Lines is a project of the Center for
the Art of Translation, a nonprofit literary
organization based in San Francisco.
To learn more about the Center, visit:
www.catranslation.org

Subscriptions
Two Lines is published twice annually.
Subscriptions are $15 per year, individual
issues are $12. To subscribe, visit:
www.twolinespress.com

Bookstores
Two Lines is distributed by
Publishers Group West, to order,
call: 1-800-788-3123

This project is supported in part by an award
from the National Endowment for the Arts.

ART WORKS.
arts.gov

Editor's Note

Choosing is the problem. It's impossible for any issue to be representative, capturing all cultures, histories, and languages, even though we work with every issue to bring more voices into *Two Lines*. But we have to choose, whether that choice is toward balance, or toward our aesthetic, or even, sometimes, pointedly against our aesthetic. We choose not to fill issues only with what we think will feel familiar to our American audience, but we also recognize that it's those same familiarities that let us (all of us) decide if we like something or not.

All editors are asked how they choose. The unsatisfying answer is that we try to find the best work we can, while both honoring and fighting against our own biases. The truer answer, although probably just as unsatisfying, is that good literature, read openly—no matter where it comes from, no matter what language it's written in, no matter what literary history it evolves from—feels honest. Close to the bone. And so, in the editorial meeting when we read Deborah Iwabuchi's translation of Nobuko Takagi's inexplicably intimate encounter with a mysterious sea creature, there's just no choice anymore. Or Tuệ Sỹ's poem that inhabits drunkenness, music, melancholia, and home in just seventeen words. Or Jeffrey Yang's essay that tracks a single story, translated over millennia and languages and, finally, into his own life. More often than not, the poems and stories that seem unlike anything we've ever read choose themselves, and we get to stand aside and let them tell you why.

—CJ EVANS

Contents

POETRY

ESSAY

Nobuko Takagi is well known for works of a sensuous nature, in particular her book Translucent Tree, *a story of love between an older couple. One of a collection of stories that was part of Kyushu University's "Soaked in Asia" project,* Tomosui *received the Kawabata Yasunari Award in 2010.*

トモスイ

春まだ浅きころ、ユヒラさんと夜釣りにでた。花芽の港から底が平たい舟でこぎ出したが、思ったほど寒くはない。

　底にはガラスが張ってあって、暗い海中がよく見える。この舟の格好が、夜釣りには最適なのだとユヒラさんは言う。なぜなら、ほら、かがり火が船底から海中にまで届くでしょう？

　それはそうだけど、とわたしはそっぽを向いた。魚屋さんで刺身を盛り合わせるハッポウスチロールの器に、二人で乗っているみたいな気がする。

「でもかがり火がない」

「今夜は月が出てますから、かがり火は要りません。月光がかがり火のかわりです」

　わたしより年若いくせに、ユヒラさんは物言うとき、唇の上にシワが寄る。強く言うときは、深いシワになる。そのあたりに本能が溜まっている気がする。月の光でも、シワが寄るのがわかる。一瞬おばあさん見える。

　そもそもユヒラさんは男らしくない。髪もふんわり丸く刈っていて、身体は小さいくせに手足の末端ばかりごつごつと大きく、けれど胸のあたりや下腹部は女のように肉付きが良い。...

Tomosui

One evening in early spring, Yuhira and I went out fishing. We left Haname Harbor in a flat-bottomed boat. It wasn't as cold as I thought it would be.

The bottom of the boat was a piece of glass, and we could see the dark sea beneath us. He thought it was the perfect boat for night fishing; sure that the boat's watch fire would reveal what was in the water below.

I supposed he was right, but I ignored him. I felt like we were in one of those Styrofoam trays fish shops use to pack purchases.

"There's no watch fire on this boat," I noted.

"There's a full moon tonight, we won't need one." Yuhira was younger than me, but when he spoke, the skin under his nose wrinkled. The more intensely he spoke, the deeper the wrinkles. Must be where his instincts collected, I thought. I could see them even in the light of the moon. They made him look like an old woman.

The thing about Yuhira was that he wasn't masculine. He was small, and he had a haircut that made a fluffy circle around his head. His hands and feet looked hard and bony, but his chest and lower abdomen seemed soft and padded, like a woman.

He occasionally went out into Haname Harbor at night, he had told me, to fish and fill up on something delicious. He'd mentioned it so many times, always promising to take me out with him, that I finally demanded he make good on his offer. He told me he usually went out alone and that I'd be the first woman he'd ever had in his boat—a fact I found oddly depressing as well as flattering. I decided it was the sort of thing that needed to be acted on quickly, and we had met at the port that night and rowed out.

I thought he'd have a hibachi on board to cook his catch, but no, he said it tasted better raw. I felt queasy thinking about eating fish straight out of the sea, but he said it wasn't fish—it was something *like* fish.

Yuhira did the rowing. He sped along as if heading for the moon hung in the middle of the sky. Ocean spray splashed over me from time to time, but it was warm. I licked the drops on my hand, and the salty taste was somehow calming. A moonlit night, I noted, was still pretty dark. The moon shown on part of the ocean surface, but the rest was colorless. I couldn't see Yuhira's face anymore. So I enjoyed imagining what his expression must look like. But when the moon-light occasionally crossed his face at an angle, I was disappointed to see that he looked the same as always.

Yuhira had informed me I was allowed to bring only a blanket, a change of clothes, and makeup onto the boat. The clothes were in case I got wet. He just had one fishing pole, the kind you could fold up until it was very small, and the bait was tucked away in his pocket. I asked him what it was, but he told me it was a surprise for later.

The gray promontory we were headed for grew longer and darker as we approached. It looked like a woman who had thrown her legs out in front of her. The tip of the headland was shaped like a foot, and the hips were covered in fog. It was all rock, but the edges were blurry, giving a soft impression.

"We're going around the point," he said.

"Yes, let's!"

"You've never been there before, have you?"

"No, it'll be the first time."

"It's a nice place."

I thought as much. We were on the sea, the moon was out, the land was shaped like a woman's legs, and I was with Yuhira. One of the reasons I liked him was that he didn't have an odor. We had kissed once for some reason, and I hadn't thought much of it because he didn't smell like a man; not his lips, mouth, face, or body. He was kind of like hot water that had been flavored by boiling broccoli in it. Ever since that kiss, I had suspected that Yuhira might not really be a man. He had a wife and children—he'd shown me a photo—but just because he had a picture of a family didn't convince me.

As we were rounding the point, a light suddenly shone on the groin area of the two legs. Yuhira said something like, "See?" and I responded enthusiastically. I was riveted by the sound of his voice; it promised something exciting up ahead.

There was a small inlet on the other side of the promontory. Blue-white moonlight shone on the trees directly surrounding it. There was no way to tell how deeply forested it was, but it looked thick and black. It was so dark below the moonlight that I couldn't even see where the trees stopped and the water began. It was all darkness, all except for that one band of light. The boat floated into it, bobbing up and down.

"We'll find it here," said Yuhira confidently.

"Is this where you're going to fish?"

"Yes, but you'd better put on some makeup first."

"But I can't see anything!"

"I've brought some candles. Just in case you fall in the ocean and die, you should at least have on some foundation and lipstick."

"I don't want to fall in."

"You won't. It'll be all right."

Like magic, Yuhira pulled several small candles and a disposable lighter out of his pocket. He lit one and dripped wax on the rim of the boat to secure it. There were eight candles in all.

I quickly applied makeup, dripping some liquid foundation into the palm of my hand, rubbing both hands together and patting it on my face just as if I were washing up. I massaged my face a little and then put on the lipstick. I could have done it without the help of the candles.

"Are you going to put on makeup, too?" I asked him.

"I think I will."

He copied me, and it just took a few minutes. Now we were even. Yes, even, and we began to banter. *We're badgers in the same hole. Badgers live in holes, so they're creatures. Are we creatures? I don't know, maybe we're snakes. No, snakes are cold. We're in the same hole together, so we need to stay warm. Or are we cold? No, we're comfortable; we're definitely badgers.*

We kept up a patter until our voices began to overlap and we couldn't hear each other anymore. I decided to stay quiet for a while.

"Well then, shall we fish?"

"Will we catch anything?"

"You must be hungry."

"Yes, a little."

Yuhira got out his collapsible fishing rod and pulled it open. He skillfully attached a line and hook. There was a breeze that played at the flames of the candles and gently rocked the boat. With every movement, the shadows fluttered on Yuhira's hands. They were deep orange with an occasional flicker of blue-green that made a mottled pattern. He quickly licked the hook with his tongue then dipped his hand into his pocket. He pulled out a ring of tamarind—it was shaped like a tiny bracelet. Tamarinds are usually long peas in a sheathe-like pod, but these were rounded, with the head and tail almost touching.

"Is this the bait?"

"It always works for me . . ."

"So, even the fish eat tamarind in this part of the world."

"I love the smell." Yuhira was thinking about the feast to come, and he swallowed in anticipation. "It tastes so good right after you haul one up—slides right down your throat."

"So you just swallow them whole?"

"Well, you'll see."

Yuhira stuck the round tamarinds onto the hook and stood up. He hopped on one foot to get his balance, and then threw the hook out into the darkness.

It wasn't weighted, but the line went out quite a distance with just the tamarind. I could see it far out as a gray spot on the black surface of the water.

It bobbed back and forth.

"All right then," Yuhira took a deep breath, "All we have to do now is wait."

For an instant, I was afraid he'd follow up "all right then" with "it's about time to die," and not having a clue about what I would do if he had, I was relieved he said something else. I had learned that he could completely upset the atmosphere with his sudden statements. He always brushed them off by saying his personality had been warped because he'd been raised in poverty. But using his childhood as an excuse was another bad habit he had, a way of ignoring what was right in front of him. I didn't think his personality was all that bad. Take that photo. He liked to give the impression it was all a lie, but they were probably his real family; his wife and children.

One day, I had thought, when I was old and if I were still friends with Yuhira, I'd confront him. *You say you don't like being a man, but you don't want to be a woman either. That's got to be harder than changing into anything in the world. If your ideal is to blend together with someone else, you'll have to go so far away that you'll lose yourself. Can someone like you, without stamina or willpower or money, pull that off?*

Now, here he was trying to do something that seemed equally

impossible: fish with a tamarind. And as I mumbled to myself, the gray spot in the distance disappeared.

"Look!" I cried.

Yuhira gave a yell too and then began to slowly reel in the line. I wanted to urge him to hurry, but he was careful. I forced myself to stay quiet. The tip of the rod twitched. We'd caught something for sure.

When the line pulled taut, the boat abruptly spun around, and the line knocked all the candles off the edge of the boat. I picked up the few that fell in the boat still lit and tossed them into the water. Now it was pitch black.

It felt as though Yuhira's catch was pulling the line here and there, but I couldn't really see it. For all I knew the boat was just going in circles. The moon had been shining to our right, but now it was dropping toward the left, casting thin rays of light onto the surface of the water.

"Are you ready?" Yuhira asked, his voice breathless. I clenched the sides of the boat, ignoring the wax that stuck to my palms, and nodded.

"Okay then, I'm going to do it, I'm really going to do it!"

"I'm ready. Come on, Yuhira, hurry!"

"Here I go!"

"Good, I'm waiting, I'm ready."

There were still flecks of light left, but it was impossible to focus on one spot; not on Yuhira as he bent and bowed, nor me as I tried to stay low.

"I think I need a break."

"No, Yuhira, I can't wait any longer."

"Okay, okay. Let me try again." He stood up again, looking brave and masculine in the moonlight. His small body was as supple as his fishing rod. He was fighting against all darkness, becoming first a bow and then a rod. "There it is! Look now, look at the bottom of the boat!"

I looked through the wet, slippery glass bottom. Yuhira had told me we wouldn't need any other light as long as we had the moon, but it was too dark to tell what was under there.

"I can't see anything."

"Sorry... It's not there anymore."

Something heavy plopped down next to me as I peered through the glass. The boat tilted, and whatever it was flopped over on top of me. Yuhira may have tried to right the balance; I wasn't sure, but the next thing I knew, I was pushed up against the other side of the boat and I could hear a whistling noise close by.

Yuhira finished winding his reel; the tamarind was still on the hook. What sort of fish would have got caught like this? I studied the wriggling mass next to me. It appeared to be neither fish nor marine plant. It was more like a shellfish without a shell, and it was about the size of a human baby. It was warm though, too warm to be a shellfish, and covered in skin that felt as smooth as leather.

As I sat there touching it and wondering how one would actually eat this naked shellfish, it continued to breathe through a tube at one end of its body.

"What is it?" I asked as Yuhira put away his fishing rod.

"People usually call it *tomosui*, but that's not its scientific name or anything."

"And you can eat it, right?"

"The flesh is tasteless, but you can suck on it to your heart's content. See those things sticking out? They've got holes in them."

I touched one end of the tomosui—it was rounded and soft like a human belly, and there was something protruding from it. On the other end was a hole, it felt like a belly button cut vertically. I touched it all over and it scrunched up and puckered out as if it were being tickled and trying to repel my hand—it was still alive. After a while, though, the tomosui seemed to give up and it went quiet.

"Well, you did it, Yuhira."

He spread out his arms as if to measure the length of the creature, and seemed satisfied with its size.

"It's the biggest one I've ever caught. There's a lot to suck there. Now I can die happy."

"No dying, please. You know you've got a bad habit of saying that every time you're thrilled by something."

"Try it! After you've had something this good, you'll feel the same way."

Yuhira flipped the tomosui over so that its "belly" was facing up. He asked me where I'd like to start, and I told him anywhere was fine. He suggested I try sucking from the tube.

I put it in my mouth, and it uncurled onto my tongue. I sucked as hard as I could. The flavor seemed strange at first, but I got used to it and began to gulp it down. With every swallow I wanted more even though I could feel it quickly filling my stomach. When I ran out of breath, I stopped to take a break but quickly put it back to my lips.

"It's delicious!" I managed to get out.

Yuhira was oblivious to me as he noisily sucked from the hole at the other end. I could hardly see where he left off and the tomosui began. In fact, he looked so happy that I asked him to let me give that end a try. He kept putting me off—*wait a sec, just one more* . . .

Finally, he flipped the tomosui around and gave me the hole. I put my mouth up to it, and there was a smell. I couldn't tell whether it belonged to the tomosui or to Yuhira. Maybe it was the combination of the lipstick and foundation we were both wearing.

Sucking from the hole took some getting used to. First you had to cover it entirely with your mouth and draw deeply. This pulled the skin around the hole into your mouth. Then you had to use your tongue to thrust the skin aside and find the lips of the hole, force them open, and finally drink.

What came out was something with the texture of unshelled eggs. I filled my mouth and then crushed them with my teeth. They were creamy and sweet, and I wanted to savor the flavor of each delicious morsel.

Every once in a while, Yuhira pulled his mouth from the tomosui and grunted. I grunted back in reply. It was all we needed to communicate. With the tomosui between us, we were a single, u-shaped body, it was impossible to tell the male from the female.

The tomosui gradually shrunk as we sucked at it from both ends.

Jan Wagner is the author of several poetry collections including Australien *(Berlin Verlag, 2010) and* Die Eulenhasser in den Hallenhäusern *(Berlin Verlag, 2012). In his native Germany he was recently honored with the Kranichsteiner Award for Literature and the Friedrich-Hölderlin-Preis literary prize.*

klatschmohn

man kann sehr lange stehen, sich gedulden,
sofern es klatschmohn gibt, seinen barocken
überschwang und jene viergeteilten
blüten zwischen weizen oder roggen,

die uns am hellen mittag plötzlich wecken,
mit allen sinnen scharf durchatmen lassen,
ein augensalmiak; kann auf den wegen
sehr lange stehen und den schatten lauschen, kann
die landschaft wie zum ersten mal erfassen,

bis alles schatten ist und juniwärme,
nurmehr der mohn sich auf die felder legt,
in leuchtkugeln herabbrennt (in der ferne

die letzte amsel und das rattern, rattern
der güterzüge), überm abend schwebt:
hier unten sind wir, niemand muß uns retten.

field poppy

you could stand here very long, patient,
as long as there's field poppy, his baroque
exuberance and those evenly quartered
blossoms in between the wheat and the rye,

so when in midday bright we jolt awake,
with all our senses fiercely breathe him in,
a seeing-salt; you can stand here on the pathways
for a very long time and listen to the shadows, the landscape,
as if just now having some realization,

until everything is shadow and june-ness;
and only the poppy out in the field is moving,
fizzling down, like flares do (while from afar,

the last blackbird and the clatter, clatter
of the freight trains) floating on the evening:
with us down here, and no one must save us.

koi

die ursuppe von teich, hinter den giebeln
der palmenhäuser: koi, wie sie sich drängen,
als goldene fäden einen gobelin

aus schwärze durchwirken, ihre bahnen
schwerer vorherzusagen als kometen;
das runde maul, das nichts als ihren namen

zu formen scheint, wenn sie den punkt berühren,
der luft von wasser trennt, ihr kammerton
zu hoch oder zu tief für unsere ohren,

unhörbar: koi, ein firmament aus geld
am grund des beckens, unter ihnen hängend,
verliebt ins schummrige wie jede glut,

neben dem plankenweg ein schweben, schwelen.
etwas von ihrer hünenhaften ruhe,
dem sturen herzschlag sollte übergehen

koi

in the primeval soup of lakes, behind the gables
of the palm houses: koi, as they clot,
as they weave into the tapestry of blackness

their golden threads, their orbits more
difficult to predict than comets;
the round mouth that seems to form

nothing but their name, touching the place
where air divides from water; their chamber pitch
too high or too low for our ears,

inaudible: koi, a firmament of coins
on the bottom of the pool, jangling beneath,
loving dimness like only embers can;

next to the promenade they hover, smoulder;
something from their hulking calm,
from their stubborn heartbeat should transfer

auf mich, wenn ich die hand ins dunkel halte
und warte auf den kalten stoß, das rauhe
paillettenkleid; und so beginnt das alter.

upon myself, when i dip my hand into the bilge
and wait for the cold jolt, the rugged gown
of sequins; thereby beginning old age.

rübezahl

bäume um bäume, und dahinter ruhig
der wald, der mit den augen seiner tiere
sieht. nur ein paar bäche infiltrieren
die dämmerung, ein dünner pfeifenrauch

von nebel steigt auf. jenseits von schreiberhau
und krummhübel: im geäst
noch immer die tropfen des gewitterschau-
ers, jeder mit dem winzigen insekt

der sonne darin, als sich die schatten
der berge strecken, du endlich die vertrauten
silhouetten der getreidesilos,

das dorf erkennst: die schädelstätte
am rand des trüben ackers nur ein haufen
von zuckerrüben, ungeheuer, zahllos.

beetcounter

After Rübezahl, an angry spirit of
spirit of the Sudeten Mountains,
literally "Beetcounter."

trees upon trees, and behind them, quietly,
dense forest, which with the eyes of his animals
sees you. only a brook intermittently
infiltrates the dusk, a thin pipe-smoke haze

of fog rising. beyond schreiberhau
and krummhübel: in the thicket,
still the drops of the thundershower,
each with the minuscule insect

of sunshine within it, as the shadows
of the mountains stretch out, and you finally reach
the familiar silhouettes of the grain silos,

the village: the cluster of skulls
at the dank field's edge, merely a bunch
of sugar beets, engorged, innumerable.

pieter codde: bildnis eines mannes mit uhr

I
kaum daß ich sie halte:
als hätte sie auf meinen fingerspitzen
sich niedergelassen, nur um kurz zu sitzen
und auszuruhen wie ein falter
von seltenem glanz,

der seine flügel öffnet, schließt,
sie öffnet, schließt,
dann golden weitertanzt.

II
ich könnte alles sein, rauhbein
und unglücksrabe, der das regennasse
gefieder schüttelt, während sein rubin
als auge in die schenke leuchtet; einer, der nur so
zum spaß zu singen anfängt, bis die pelzigen raupen
des schnurrbarts tanzen unter seiner nase;

ein tulpenspekulant, ein reeder,
der sich versteckt hält hinter butzenscheiben,

pieter codde: portrait of a man with watch

I
less do i hold this thing
than over my fingers it lies
having lowered itself, momentarily
at rest like butterfly wings
of rare brilliance,

which open, close,
and then open, close,
then, goldenly, dance.

II
i could be anything, could be the roughneck,
could be the birdbrain shaking off his rain-wet
plumage, while his ruby-ring
blazes like an eye before a lantern;
one who willy-nilly starts to sing,
which makes the caterpillar mustache dance;

a tulip-gambler, a headshipman,
who hides himself behind crown glass windows,

von reisen träumt nach ceylon und retour,
während die kannen in den höfen scheppern,
die kühlen milchlaternen haarlems oder rotter-
dams. vernehme ich im schlaf das schaben

der taue? muß ich weinen, wenn die graugän-
se weiterziehen, ist mein wams benetzt
von rauch und pulver dutzender von kriegen?
ich könnte alles sein, opportunist
und ränkeschmied—der runde, weiße kragen
aus seide kunstvoll wie ein wespennest.

III
wieder geht dein blick
zurück zu dem detail: du siehst den bart
am kinn, das grau darin, und den bestick-
ten ärmelschlitz; du siehst die borte

am umgeklappten hemd, wo flocke
um flocke schnee vernäht ist, und die schläfe,
von der die locke hängt wie eine flagge
jenseits der grenze, ohne winde, schlaff.

mein breitkrempiger hut, der wie ein loch
dahinter klafft, ein tintenfäßchen
das umgekippt ist, dessen lache

sich langsam ausdehnt, deren schwarz mich einsaugt,
während das auge spricht: bleib noch ein bißchen,
perfekter falter, tickendes insekt.

dreaming of the journeys to ceylon,
while the churns in the courtyards clatter:
cool milk-lanterns of haarlem or rotterdam.
do i hear in my sleep the scraping ropes

of ships? must i cry, when the gray geese
move on, is my doublet dusted
with the smoke and powder of dozens of wars?
i could be everything, opportunist
and intriguer—the round, white collar
of silk, as elaborate as a wasp's nest.

III
again your gaze must follow
back to the details: you see my beard
on the chin, the gray within, and the embroidered
sleeve with a vent; you see the border

of the folded-up shirt, where flake
after flake of snow is sewn on, and the temple,
from which a curl hangs like a flag
beyond its frontier, without wind, limp.

and my broad-brimmed hat that like a hole
yawns behind me, an inkpot,
recently knocked over, whose puddle

slowly spreads outward, whose black
absorbs me while the eye says: stay like that,
perfect butterfly, ticking insect.

Christos Ikonomou is a fiction writer, journalist, and translator living in Athens. Something Will Happen, You'll See, *which won the most prestigious literary award for Greek fiction in 2010, and his latest book,* All Good Things Will Come from the Sea, *are both forthcoming in English translation from Archipelago Books.*

Κάτι θα γίνει, θα δεις

Σήμερα έστειλαν κι άλλη ειδοποίηση απ' την τράπεζα. Γράφουν ότι είναι η τελευταία και ότι την άλλη βδομάδα θα προχωρήσουν στις «προβλεπόμενες από τον νόμο ενέργειες». Τηλεφώνησαν κιόλας πολλές φορές αλλά η Νίκη δεν απάντησε. Άφησε το χαρτί στο τραπεζάκι του σαλονιού. Όταν γύρισε ο Άρης απ' τη δουλειά του 'ριξε μια ματιά αλλά δεν είπε τίποτα. Ούτε τ' ακούμπησε καν. Στεκόταν μονάχα και το κοίταγε με μάτια μαραμένα απ' το ξενύχτι. Ακούρευτος, αξύριστος, οι φαβορίτες του κατέβηκαν μέχρι το λαιμό και μοιάζει σαν λυκάνθρωπος. Ύστερα έβγαλε τις μπότες του και πήγε στην κρεβατοκάμαρα κι έπεσε με τα ρούχα στο κρεβάτι και τράβηξε το σεντόνι ψηλά πάνω απ' το κεφάλι του.

Τρεις ώρες τώρα στο κρεβάτι. Αμίλητος. Ακίνητος. Θαρρείς πως σταμάτησε κιόλας ν' αναπνέει.

Η Νίκη βάζει πλυντήριο κι ύστερα βάζει σκούπα και σφουγγαρίζει. Σκύβει στα γόνατα και μαζεύει τα σπασμένα γυαλιά κάτω απ' το τραπέζι της κουζίνας. Το πάτωμα μυρίζει τσίπουρο. Ρίχνει κι άλλο απορρυπαντικό και το τρίβει με δύναμη ώσπου τα δάχτυλά της ασπρίζουν και πονάνε. Μια στο τόσο έρχεται στην πόρτα της κρεβατοκάμαρας και τον κοιτάει, περιμένει να δει πόσο θ' αντέξει....

Something Will Happen, You'll See

Another notification came today from the bank. It says it's a final notification and that next week they'll take "actions permitted by law." They've called several times too but Niki never picks up. She set the letter on the coffee table in the living room. When Aris came home from work he saw it but didn't say anything. He didn't even touch it. He just stood and looked at it with eyes glazed from lack of sleep. Unshaven, in need of a haircut, his sideburns as long as a werewolf's. Then he took off his shoes and went into the bedroom and collapsed fully dressed onto the bed and pulled the sheet up over his head.

He's been lying there for three hours. Not speaking. Not moving. You'd think he even stopped breathing.

Niki loads the washing machine, then vacuums and mops. She gets down on all fours to pick up the broken glass from under the kitchen table. The floor smells of tsipouro. She douses it with disinfectant and scrubs until her fingers turn white and start to ache. Every so often she goes over to the bedroom door and looks at him, wondering how long he'll last.

You'll suffocate in there, she finally says. Come on out. You're not going to achieve anything that way.

No response. But Niki knows he's listening. His left leg is quaking under the sheet. As if he had no control over it—as if it were someone else's leg, not his.

You have to stay strong, she says. Something will happen, you'll see. Banks don't just take people's homes away. This isn't America. We'll manage somehow. You'll see.

Outside the sun is starting to set. The sunlight has cast an orange patch on the wall over the bed. Niki stares at it, wondering how she never noticed that orange patch on the wall before. She thinks how unfair it is that she doesn't know what to say to Aris, to make him understand how it feels to be seeing that patch on the wall for the very first time. Last night after helping him to bed she made herself some coffee and turned on the television. Recently she'd been having trouble sleeping and Aris was snoring so loudly that she knew even if she lay down she wouldn't be able to sleep. There was a documentary on about American Indians but Niki just stared out through the balcony door at the glow from the floodlights over at the electric plant. That afternoon a bunch of workers had climbed up on the chimney and hung a banner and shouted slogans. She watched the beams from the floodlights slicing the darkness like enormous swords and wondered how an artist would paint this scene—if there were still artists left in the world who painted scenes like that: a woman sitting in the dark with a cup of coffee and a cigarette, her face lit by the dim blue light of the television. Wouldn't be much of a painting. Maybe if she had a gun in her hand, or a vibrator. Coffee and cigarettes didn't cut it. People don't get excited anymore about old-fashioned things. Who cares about the finances and family problems of the petite bourgeoisie? Très banal. She leaned over to stub out her cigarette and saw a girl on TV who looked like an Indian only she was wearing glasses and modern clothes and talking about the history of her tribe and saying that many many years ago the people of her tribe had been forced to leave their land and as they left some touched the leaves and branches as a way of saying good-bye and others touched the grass and the flowers and the water that bubbled from the springs and the pebbles on the riverbanks, and the soldiers who had come to force them out had watched this peculiar sight and laughed—they didn't know what it's like to have to leave a place you love, the girl said. The interviewer asked how she knew about all those things if they'd happened so long ago and the girl said that the truth of a story lies not in its adherence to the facts but in its moral character. When the documentary was over Niki turned off the television opened the balcony door and looked at the beams from the flashlights of the striking workers at the electric plant who seemed prepared to spend all night perched up there on the chimney and as she looked at the dark shapes of the brick buildings and the exhaust tower she remembered her mother saying that in her day all the doctors in that area used to tell new mothers not to breastfeed their babies because the air in those neighbor-hoods—Haravgi Drapetsona Keratsini—was full of fluorine from the fertilizer plant in Drapetsona and the fluorine got into their milk. Then she went into the bedroom and looked at her husband who was sleeping wrapped up in the sheet with his socks still on and she pulled a jacket over her shoulders and took her coffee and cigarettes and keys and went upstairs onto the roof of the building and looked down at the world spread out all around her. The port the ships the housing projects. The abandoned fertilizer plant the chim-neys the water towers. The sky was full of stars and the moon was out but Niki didn't need any light to see—even with her eyes closed she knew where everything was. The cement factory the slaughter-houses the British Petroleum plant the church of Agios Nikolas. The fishing docks and the boatyards in Perama. In the distance was the industrial island of Psyttaleia and then Salamina with its densely clustered neighborhoods: Paloukia Ambelakia Selinia. She grabbed hold of the railing and felt its rough metal scratch her palms. From where she stood she could see the memorial to the battle against the

Germans at the electric plant in 1944 which was now surrounded by palm trees and she could see countless unnamed alleys and streets lined with bitter orange trees and mulberry trees and apartment buildings built side by side whose balcony awnings were torn by wind and blackened with age. Her gaze wandered back down to the cars and motorbikes and motorized tricycles and the yards in front of the refugee houses, yards with flowerpots and clothes strung up on lines and old useless things—a broken refrigerator, a bicycle with no wheels, a three-legged chair, a crib with no slats. Then she looked back at the apartment buildings and at the lighted windows here and there and wondered if other people were up as late as she was tonight or if they'd left those lights on out of fear. And if they were still awake was it because of something good or something bad? And if they'd left the lights on out of fear what were they afraid of? Burglars, or something else? She lit a cigarette and drank her coffee which had grown cold and looked around again and wondered what she would do if one day she was forced to leave this place, the place where she was born and raised and became a woman. If she would go out into the street and say good-bye to the bitter orange trees and mulberry trees by touching their leaves and their branches. If she would touch all the park benches in all the squares and all the utility poles plastered with posters and funeral announcements and For Rent signs. And the red Vespa still chained to the front gate of Thodoris Skoupas's yard, which he washed every Sunday morning while he was alive and then doused with cologne to make it smell nice. You'd think she was an Indian the way she would run her hands over the metal grate on Asterias's newspaper stand, which had been closed for years now—run and hide Asterias the anarchists are coming, the kids used to yell who hated him because of the big AEK team poster he'd hung behind the counter. She would touch the wall at the corner of Bosphorus and Mycenae Streets across from the school where a line of faded spray-paint read *vacation is the alibi for an eleven-month rape.* And the front gate of Voula's house that's been crooked since the night last year when her husband came home drunk and drove right into it. She would touch the window of Kosmas's barbershop where one afternoon twenty years ago she had seen a fifteen-year-old Aris sitting in the chair with his head bowed and his hair in tufts on the floor around him—and how dearly she wishes she could turn back time and sweep all that hair off the floor into her hand and smooth it back onto Aris's head.

There were so many things she would have to touch in farewell if one day she were forced to leave this place. Even if she isn't an Indian and there aren't soldiers to watch her and laugh even if there isn't anyone to tell her story on television.

And now she's standing at the bedroom door looking at Aris and that orange patch on the wall and remembering all the things she heard last night on TV. The truth of a story lies not in its adherence to the facts but in its moral character. She's not sure exactly what that means but she does like to think there might be true things that have never happened. She likes to think there are things that are both true and not true. Things that may never have happened but are still truer than the truth. Then again she isn't sure. If only she could understand better. If only they had money and she didn't have to work. If only she could read more and travel and go to the theater and concerts. If only she could sleep until eleven and not have to wait before dawn at the bus stop and be ashamed of her job. More than anything she would like not to feel a shock of fear every time the phone rings or she sees a plain white envelope in the mailbox.

She lies down beside Aris and the bed squeaks.

Come on out, she says to him. I want to tell you something. It happened at work yesterday. You've never heard anything like it.

No reaction. Niki turns onto her back and closes her eyes. She recalls the images to mind, tries to put them in order and make the lump in her throat go away. She lets her heart grow cold. The story she wants to tell is a love story and she knows that kind of story can't be told with a warm heart.

Around eleven I take a cigarette break and Rita comes whirling into the room and says listen to this you're not going to believe what happened you're going to flip. What happened, I say. Did one of the doctors ask you out? You know how Rita's been dying to hook a doctor or an army officer ever since she was a girl. Shut up and listen, she says, this is for real. Earlier this morning they brought in this couple from the Korydallos prison in an ambulance. The girl was one of ours and the guy was a foreigner. Bulgarian or Romanian I don't know. A young couple. He got locked up and she went to see him during visiting hours. In a few days they were going to send him back to his country, to deport him, you know. So during visiting hours this girl takes a tube of glue out from somewhere some kind of superglue and smears it all over her hand and they stick their hands together just like that. See? So they could be together forever and she could always stick by her man. Can you believe it? They stuck their hands together with superglue so that no one could tear them apart. Unbelievable. Just imagine, the things that happen in this world. Isn't it crazy? And now they brought them here so the doctors can get their hands apart. They took them up to the second floor. You know, to that room where they put the convicts. They've even got a guard up there keeping watch. It happened just now. Can you imagine, gluing their hands together. I'll bet they're some kind of addicts. Good riddance, I say, we don't need their kind around here.

That's what Rita says and then she takes a few drags of my cigarette and goes back to work all annoyed because a guy on her floor keeps throwing up—goddamned old man she says to me, he's been running me ragged since morning.

Niki rolls onto her side and looks at Aris. Wrapped in the sheet, arms at his sides, his breath barely audible, like a whisper.

Did you get what happened? she asks him. They stuck their hands together with glue so that no one could tear them apart. What do you think of that?

She looks at the sheet which has taken on the shape of his face. Then she lifts her head and looks at the orange spot on the wall which is shrinking smaller and smaller as the sunlight fades. She reaches out a hand and touches it before it vanishes altogether. She takes a breath and closes her eyes again.

I take my bucket and mop and go up to the second floor. I don't know what came over me. I wanted to see them. I wanted to see how it was, I wanted to see them. That room for the convicts is at the very end of the hallway by the bathrooms. There's a young policeman sitting in front of the door smoking and playing with his cell phone. He sees me coming with my gear and I figure he won't let me in—he looks me over from head to toe. He makes me wait for a while then waves me in as if shooing a fly.

The room has an iron door with a padlock and a single bed and a window with bars and screens. Just like a cell. We don't clean it much. I've probably only been in there two or three times. The young man is lying on the bed. Naked from the waist up with his eyes closed and his right hand on his chest. His left hand is joined to the right hand of the girl who's sitting next to him on the edge of the bed and staring out the window. I can't see their hands because they're wrapped in gauze. Rita was right they're just kids. Twenty, twenty-two at the most. But they don't look like addicts—at least not the girl. When I go into the room the guy opens his eyes and looks at me vacantly then sighs and shuts his eyes again. But the girl smiles and stands up. Her skirt has crept up over her knees and she smooths it down with her free hand. Her cheeks are bright red.

Sorry to bother you, I say. I won't be long.

I start cleaning taking my time in no hurry at all. Of course what is there to clean in there really. I keep on glancing over to see what they're up to trying to think of something to say. I think about asking if she's okay what the doctors said how many days they're going to keep them in the hospital if they're going to operate stuff like that. I want to ask if it was her idea for them to stick their hands together what kind of glue she used what the guards and prison officials did when they found out. Like if they hit her or yelled at her. There are so many things I want to ask. But I'm afraid the guard might hear us talking and kick me out. Besides I figure they might not be in the mood to talk. She's having a pretty rough time as it is the last thing she needs is some cleaning lady she doesn't even know peppering her with questions.

As I'm mopping I hear the young man murmur something. The girl bends down and strokes his forehead and hair. Then she turns and asks in a whisper if I have any cigarettes. Of course, I whisper back, and pull out my pack. She takes one and lights it and puts it in the kid's mouth. I gesture to her to keep the whole pack. Take it, I say, I've got another downstairs. I ask her if they need anything else. If she wants me to call a nurse or bring them some water or something from the canteen. I tell her I've brought stuffed tomatoes from home and feta and bread but I don't know if the guard will let me give it to them.

We're fine, she says with a smile and blushes even more. Thank you so much. We're fine. Thank you.

And then a strange thing happens. There we are talking in whispers and gestures and she suddenly holds out her hand to me. I don't know why I hesitate. I don't know why but I hesitate to take her hand. It's true. I stand there like an idiot holding my mop and staring at the hand she's stretched out in my direction. It's a tiny hand, like a drop of water. White and thin.

The girl smiles but in a kind of crooked way. Like when you get an injection at the dentist's office that makes your mouth all numb and swollen. Then she leans toward me and—

Don't worry, she whispers. There's no glue on this one.

The sunlight has faded even more now. Through the balcony door Niki sees the streetlights coming on with a cautious flutter. The cars passing by in the street have their lights on now. The room grows darker, filling with a strange darkness that seems almost alive.

That's all, Niki says. Then I went downstairs and worked until three and came home. I wanted to tell you about it last night but last night you weren't in such great shape, as I'm sure you remember. Do you? Do you remember anything about last night? Falling asleep at the kitchen table? With your cigarette still burning? You almost lit yourself on fire.

Aris says something but his voice is swallowed up by the sheet.

What did you say? I can't hear you. Come on out from under there already.

Her hands are sweaty. She wipes them on the sheet and looks at her palms. Then at her fingers. For the first time she notices how yellow they are. She's been smoking too much recently. Her fingers seem smaller, too. It must be her imagination but she's terrified by even the thought that her body has started to fall apart, to shrink. In the past she would have laughed at the idea. She would have told Aris: look at this, my fingers are shrinking. I've actually been working my fingers to the bone. And they would have laughed. They would have put their hands together to see how much bigger his fingers were than hers. Then Aris would have grabbed them one by one and tugged on them to make them longer. They would laugh and laugh. But now Niki is afraid. There are so many small tiny things that frighten her. And then there's that pain in her chest. As if something in there is broken. As if something in there broke or got knocked out of place. She can feel some hard thing hanging in her chest like a broken spring. She observes the lines carved into her palms. Too many to count. Straight and crooked and curved. Some like barbed wire others like uprooted trees. Still others cross one another and fade away, or stop suddenly like a road that dead ends into nothingness.

You should have called the stations.

Aris has pulled the sheet down from over his head and is looking at her. White as a ghost, lips dry, eyes bloodshot. His hair sticking up on one side like the plume on the helmet of an ancient warrior emerging from a bloody battle.

About what?

You should have called the stations, Aris says and turns his face away. They'd kill for that kind of news. You know, human interest stories. They would have gone nuts. You should have called and told them to come to the hospital and then asked to be paid for giving them the scoop. They would have given you something for sure. Even a little would have helped in our situation. Better than nothing.

He rubs his eyes then slips his hands under his head. He stares up at the darkening ceiling.

Niki can't see his hands.

She gets up out of the bed and goes over to the balcony door. Now the sky is a dark violet color. She sees a few stars flicker and the lights of an airplane slowly disappear. The banner is still hanging from the chimney of the electric plant but tonight there are no floodlights or striking workers. The strike was deemed illegal, they said on TV. Tonight things are calm again. All that's left is the banner hanging from the chimney, a long, narrow white banner with red letters which if you saw it from a distance, from the sea, would look like a huge gauze bandage spotted with blood.

You should have called the stations, Aris says. Now it's too late.

Niki looks at her palms and recalls that image once more. The girl in the hospital. How she leaned forward with one hand stuck to the young man's and the other extended toward Niki. The thin white hand Niki was afraid to touch. She wanted to do something for that girl. Something, anything. But now there was no point. She'll learn to live with that. Compromise. All of life is one big compromise. We're all born of compromise, Niki thinks, out of that great silent yes that our parents say when they choose to bring us into this world. Which means that we all carry a kind of compromise inside us, in our blood. That's why all revolutions are destined to fail. Then she thinks how she shouldn't waste time thinking about things like that. She should think instead about how she's going to find money and about the bank and the house and Aris who is still lying under the sheet—unspeaking unmoving defeated. She thinks that if things go wrong, if they don't find some way, she'll take some superglue and stick one of her hands to Aris's and the other to the wall. That's what she'll do. Then let them come and try to kick her and Aris out of the house. This isn't America. They can come if they want. She and Aris will be waiting.

She might even call the stations.

In the distance she sees a boat steaming off with all its lights on. A woman walks by in the street pushing a baby in a stroller. Two men stand talking on the sidewalk. One is smoking and the other is carrying a fishing pole and a blue plastic bag.

And then she doesn't want to see anything or think anything anymore. She closes her eyes and leans on the glass of the balcony door and with her eyes closed listens to the darkness of the house spreading itself around her and listens to the heartless hum of cars down below in the street.

Behzad Zarrinpour is one of the most notable contemporary avant-garde poets in Iran. Zarrinpour was born in 1968 in the city of Khorramshahr, Iran. He was an editor of Zan Daily, *an arts and literature magazine banned in 1999, and of* Asia Daily, *banned in 2003.*

خرمشهر و تابوتهای بی در و پیکر /بهزاد زرین پور

برای برادرم بهروز که کارون تمامش را پس نداد

آن وقت ها که دستم به زنگ نمی رسید
در می زدم
حالا که دستم به زنگ می رسد
دیگر دری نمانده است.
بر می گردم:

یکی دو روز مانده به زنگ های تفریح
"برنامه ی کودک" تازه تمام شده
و ما مثل همیشه توپ را می بریم که...
طنین کشدار سوتی غریب
بازی را متوقف کرد
صدای گنجشک ها را برید
جنین کال زنی بر زمین افتاد
کارون یک لحظه زیر پل ایستاد
و ما به بازی جدیدی دعوت شدیم

Lidless Coffins with No Bodies

In Khorram-shahr, for my brother Behrooz.
The Caroun river did not return him to us.

I couldn't reach the bell
so I used to knock.
Now that I can reach it
the door isn't there anymore.
I return:

It's a day or two before
the ringing of school bells,
the children's TV show
has just ended and as usual
we pick up the ball
when
an elastic eerie siren
stops our play,
lacerates the finches' chirps.
A woman's unripe fetus
falls to the ground.
The Caroun river halts

که توپ هایش به جای گل آتش می شدند

گنجشک ها لانه هایشان را پایین آوردند

ما بادبادک هایمان

و بزرگترها صدایشان را.

از آن پس دیگر

زیر هیچ سقفی سفره پهن نشد.

پیراهنم را در می آورم

کارون مرا به جا نمی آورد

رفتار تلخ آب

اجساد باد کرده را

از ذهن او به فراموشی دریا ریخت

انگار جز ماتم از این رود چیزی نمی توان گرفت.

بر می گردم:

بابای خط خورده ی مدرسه مان را

از زیر آوار دفتر بیرون میکشند

در یک دستش نقشه ایران مچاله شده

و در دست دیگرش

دستمالی مانده از رقصها و گریه های محلی.

و ما با کمال وحشت و بغض های طبیعی

نمی توانستیم از تعطیلی مدرسه تا اطلاع ثانوی خوشحال نباشیم

روی میزهای ما تقویم جدیدی گذاشتند

که تمام روزهایش تا اطلاع ثانوی قرمز بود.

به تیمار نخلهای سر خورده می روم

طناب می طلبند از من

for a moment
beneath the bridge
and we are invited
to a new game where balls
transpose to flames
instead of flowers.

The finches lower their nests,
we reel in our kites,
the grown-ups hush their voices,
and from then on
no tablecloths are spread
for meals.

I take off my shirt.
Caroun river does not remember me.
Water treats bloated bodies
bitterly, dumps them
out of the river's memory
into the ocean's oblivion.
It is as if
the river could yield nothing
but mournful grief.
I return:

They pull our school's caretaker,
a deleted man,
out from under the rubble
of headmaster's office,
one hand clasping
a crumpled map of Iran,
the other a kerchief

چقدر شانه هایشان سوخته در حسرت <<تاب>>

و هنوز روزهای جمعه، سایه هایشان را تمییز می کنند.

بر میگردم

که تاب بیاورم:

باد مشام شهر را پر از بوی انهدام کرده است

هیچ کس از ملامت آفتاب

به ملایمت بی اعتبار دیوارها پناه نمی برد

سفره هاي بي تعارف

وعده های توخالی

شکم هایی که جای نان گلوله می خورند

و نمکی های ورشکسته ای

که گونی هایشان را برای ساختن سنگر به جبهه فرستادند

وحشت، زبان مادربزرگ را چنان گرفته بود

که نمازهای ناخوانده اش را درست به جا نمی آورد

و آن ها که از ما کمی بزرگتر بودند

تفنگ ها و خیالهای ساده شان را بر می داشتند

و برای پس گرفتن خواب ها و رنگ های پریده ما

تا مرز باران و دیوانگی پیش می رفتند

و چند گلوله بعد

میان مصراعی شکسته تشییع می شوند

و ما که دیگر قافیه ای برای باختن نداشتیم

مرثیه های سپید می سرودیم.

تا مادر در خانه را قفل کند

for local dances and tears.
And we, despite our normal
terror and fury, cannot contain
our joy in closing of schools
until further notice.
We are given new calendars,
every day of which is marked
in red *until further notice.*

I go to care for injured palm
trees. They ask me for ropes.
How their shoulders are burnt
in their longing for swings,
and how every Friday they
sweep the shadows of these palms.

I return
to bring them swings.

The wind has filled the city's nostrils
with destruction's odor.
No one flees the harsh sun
for the gentleness of unstable walls.
Spread-out inhospitable tablecloths,
empty promises,
stomachs that instead of bread
eat bullets,
and bankrupt salt sellers
who have dispatched their gunnysacks
to the war front to be swelled with sand.
Grandmother's tongue is so terror-struck
she cannot remember her prayers.

پدر در قفس را گشود
اما <<کاکا یوسف>>
بی اعتنا از کنار درخت ها گذشت...
و این ابتدای غربت و جیره بندی ماه
و امتداد شب های بی خیر و پنجره زیر خیمه هایی بود
که جا به اندازه کافی برای خواب های بی جای ما نداشتند.

روزهای اول
همه نماز و خیمه شان را شکسته برپا کردند
و هر جا می رفتند
کلید خانه شان را هم با خود می بردند
یادشان رفته بود
که پشت پایمان کسی آب نریخت
وقتی شهر را با خودش تنها میگذاشتیم.

تمام این سال ها
دلم یکپارچه آهن شده بود
غیر از محله کودکی ام
هیچ چیز نمی توانست بربایدش
اما حالا دیگر چگونه می توان
سر به هوا میان کوچه ها و میدان های «مین» دوید
و با شیطنت از روی آتشی پرید
که برای سوزاندن برپا شده است؟

چقدر بهانه می گیرم
من که این همه سال

Boys a bit older than us
pick up guns and birdbrained ideas
and march to the borders of rain and lunacy
to reclaim our lost sleep and vanished colors;
and after a few bullets are buried
amidst a few broken verses.

And we who didn't have the opportunity
to lose our rhyme, instead compose
shroud-white elegies.

By the time mother locked the doors
father had unlatched the cage,
but our pigeon journeyed
past the trees, unperturbed . . .
And this
was the beginning of exile
and of rationing of the moon,
the continuation of bountyless
nights, windowless tents too small
for our dislocated dreams.

Those first days
everyone raised their tents
and prayers halfheartedly.
They carried their house keys
everywhere they went,
forgetting that when we had left
the city alone on its own
no one had sprinkled blessing-water
behind our departing steps.

چنان فقیر و سربه زیر خواب دیده ام
که یک ریال بهانه به دست هیچ کس نداده ام
فقط دلم می خواهد
دوباره با پول های توجیبی ام قلک بگیرم
اما این بار از گلوله و گندم پرش کنم
اما این بار...
صدای باد در می آید
حس می کنم حرف های زیادی برای وزیدن دارد.

انگشتم را خیس می کنم
و بی جهت دنبال باد می وزم:

ساعت های عقب مانده
تفریح های زنگ خورده در حیاط مدرسه
نرده های درو شده
بذرهای عمل نکرده
نخل های روانی
عروسک هایی با آرایش نظامی یکدست
بانک هایی که خون در حساب هایشان جاریست
تابوتهای بی در و پیکر
شیروانی های بی پرو بال
ناودان های گرفته یی که در مرز بریدگی
هنوز احتمال بارندگی به کوچه می دهند
پنجره های وامانده
دیوارهای شکست خورده
و کوچه های له شده یی
که خیال بلند شدن ندارند

Through the years
my heart became a slab of steel
that nothing could cut through
except for my childhood turf.
But now how could we run
carefree through its mine-filled
streets and squares,
or impishly jump over bonfires
set not for play but to scorch?

How I fret,
I, who for all these years
dreamed so humbly
and with such privation
as to not give a soul
a cent's worth of claim.
All I want is to spend
my pocket money on a piggy bank
—except that this time
I'd fill it with bullets and wheat.
This time . . .
The wind's voice rises.
I sense it has much talk to blow.

I wet my finger and run aimlessly
with the wind:

Clocks that always tick behind,
schoolyards' rusted-bell recesses,
harvested fences,
unsowed seeds,
jittery palm trees,

انگار هیچوقت چراغان نبوده اند.
برادرم بهروز
در خیال های پرداخت نخورده اش
از این که کوچه یی به نامش خواهد شد
چقدر راضی بود
همیشه می گفت
دلم برای آنها که بی کوچه می میرند می سوزد.

آی کوچه ها، کوچه ها کدامتان
تا همیشه بلند می مانید؟
آآی ی...
کاروان خوش گل و لای
به ماهیان موج گرفته ات بگو
با بلم های به ماتم نشسته کنار بیایند
فسیل رقصهای له شده را
از زیر آوار پل به موزه نمی برند.

dolls in full military makeup,
banks with accounts liquid with blood,
lidless coffins with no bodies,
roof gables without feathers and wings,
blocked drain pipes that even on the edge
of brokenness will the possibility
of spurting into the streets,
windows left ajar,
broken walls and pummeled streets
that have no desire to rise
as if never festooned with lamps.

My brother Behrooz,
in his yet unpaid fancies
was satisfied that an alley
would be named after him.
He'd always say: *I pity those who die
without such promise of a backstreet.*

Backstreets and alleys,
which one of you will remain
erect and standing?
Aye, aye,
prodigious Caroun river,
tell your shell-stunned fish
to reconcile with these boats
that grief-sway on the shores.
The fossils of scales and
pummeled dances are not rescued
from under the collapsed bridge
to be ferried off to museums.

And Thirst

> *Transmigration is wilderness, passion is thirst.*
> —Bodhiruci II, Ratnamegha Sutra, seventh century AD

The Ratnamegha Sutra, or Jewel Rain Sutra, was presented to Empress Wu Zetian in the year 693 by Bodhiruci, a sramana from the south of India, who was invited to China at the request of the Empress. *Sramana*, a wandering Buddhist ascetic, means "one who exerts," or "one who strives," in the practice of the eight flowers and the nine-fold path. A colophon on the Dunhuang Caves manuscript of the Ratnamegha Sutra lists thirty people who were involved in the preparation of the Chinese translation, which included nine translators from India, along with expounders of the Sanskrit and Chinese, co-expounders, philologists, assistant philologists, proofreaders, and copiers. Empress Wu's reign lasted fifteen years, a period known as the second Zhou Dynasty, a brief disruption in the middle of the Tang. As the only female emperor in Chinese history, she identified herself as the Bodhisattva Maitreya, a figure thought to be male in a female apparitional form. The translation of the Jewel Rain Sutra included interpolated text that welcomed Empress Wu as the ruler of Jambudvipa, the island-continent of the terrestrial world.

Comment se souvenir de la soif? the wandering cinematographer Sandor Krasna asks in Chris Marker's film *Sans soleil.*

How can one remember thirst?

Krasna is only an apparition, never on screen, not even a voice. A moment before, he called remembering "the inner lining of forgetting," as the landscape below passed through a porthole plane, tributaries surface like the folds of a brain.

Comment se souvenir de la soif?

These words from a letter read aloud by a female narrator to the continuous sound of flowing water and the image of a woman, perhaps from the Bijago Archipelago, perhaps Bissau, sitting in a wooden motorboat moving across foamy water. Her face turns from sunlight and sea to glance at the camera, then quickly turns away, frame and profile face, gaze away, arms on knees, hand rises, shot freezes: time stilled. It is the only frozen frame in Marker's film, and lasts for an instant, barely noticeable, the inverse effect of the miraculous moment in *La jetée* when *la femme* suddenly opens her eyes and wakes, a parenthetical moment, as what comes before and after is composed of narration over photo stills because, as Marker once said, at the time he couldn't afford any reel. But the woman in the boat is not an actor—to the viewer she's anonymous, a stranger in the real. Wherefrom and whereto not revealed.

At the sign, at the limit, bounded by forest, by waters.

That we may through life advance towards the mark thou hast set before us . . .

In the space of that one brief frame, in the still, a visual correspondence can be recalled across time and place to a very old conception of the universe. Textual scholars tell us that the idea of *wu xing* 五行, the five elemental phases of traditional Chinese alchemy, was already common in the kingdom of Han during the second century BC. Fire, water, wood, metal, and earth—the perpetual cycling of *qi* 氣 (matter-breath-energy) through the five phases correlates all nature, organic processes, physiological and biological processes, as well as individual and social conduct, arts, and politics. When the four pillars were broken and the world was in chaos, the goddess Nüwa patched the sky by smelting together the five-colored stones. Earth is yellow, wood is bluegreen, metal is white, fire is red, water is black. Water produces wood, wood produces fire, fire produces earth, earth produces metal, metal produces water. Metal is autumn, water is winter, wood is spring, fire is summer, earth is midsummer. Wood overcomes earth, earth overcomes water, water overcomes fire, fire overcomes metal, metal overcomes wood. Fire is the vermilion bird, metal is the white tiger, earth is the yellow dragon, wood is the bluegreen dragon, water is the dark warrior. Refining earth produces wood, refining wood produces fire, refining fire produces clouds of metallic 氣, refining clouds of metallic 氣 produces water, refining water reverts to earth. Earth is the marking cord, metal is the square, water is the weight, wood is the compass, fire is the balance beam. Water is north, metal is west, earth is the center, fire is south, wood is east. Water to harmonize earth, earth to harmonize fire, fire to transform metal, metal to rule wood, wood reverts to earth. Wood is the eyes, fire is the nose, earth is the mouth, metal is the ears, water is the tongue. And so on with flavors, visceral orbs, crops, offices, musical notes, spirits, planets, stems, branches, lunar lodges, *yang* and *yin*.

The five phases interact together and so, useful things are brought to completion, says the *Huainanzi*, the Daoist manual of the Liu clan.

In Marker's frozen frame, each of the five elemental phases is represented in one resonant image that echoes Krasna's question, an aural mandala in the age of digital production, centered around the anonymous Bijago woman:

sunlight → fire (south)
sea → water (north)
boat → wood (east)
camera (that sees unseen) → metal (west)
earth → thirst (center and voice)

"Thirst," from the Old English *purst* from West Germanic *thurstus* from Proto-Germanic *thurs-* from Proto-Indo-European *ters-* meaning "dry; to dry"—the asterisk a linguistic signifier of hypothetical, reconstructed forms of Indo-European, that weirdly diverse family of languages that links English with ancient Greek, Latin, Hittite, Vedic Sanskrit, Pali, Avestan, Celtic, and Norse-Germanic, along with the dozens of modern sub-splinterings, from Bengali to Urdu to Persian to Pashto to Armenian, Latvian, Czech, Russian, Danish, Welsh, the Romantics, and on and between. We're told that the Proto-Indo-Europeans—the parent-progenitors of our language—lived sometime during the fourth millennium BC, as Stone Age shifted to Bronze Age, somewhere in the Caucasus Mountains or at the northern tip of the Caspian Sea or North of the Black Sea or in Anatolia, in a mythical land Wendy Doniger has called "east of the asterisk," or what can be imagined as east of the Greek *asteriskos*, or "little star."

Tract of earth our thirst.

Robert Bresson described cinematography as "continually believing." What arises from the passing frames of a film is the "illusion of an impossible lived experience," which Levi-Strauss compares to the quick repetition and accumulation of ritual. Poetry, while rooted in ritual, displaces the illusion with an actualized experience, the unconscious data of experience—allusions offscreen, its images not fixed in a single narrative. *Sans soleil* is a film that unfolds as one kind of poetic experience, with its lyrical linkages across cultures and histories, its echoes of predecessors and structural rhymes, its narrative alternatives. A frozen frame of film becomes a photograph, a fragment of perception, beckoning the past with memory, reverberations of *soif*. The Bijago woman in the boat in the sun on the water, we watch, a moment of her journey, as she sits in anticipation of a destination. Memory traces in language to an as yet unknown beginning of **ters-*. Lévi-Strauss, quoting Franz Boas who quoted a Tsetsaut slave of the Nisga'a, tells us that for the Tsetsauts, who lived in what became British Columbia and were extinct by 1895, the terrestrial world was flat, hot, and dry, with no water. Hunger and thirst reigned, until the animals tore up the celestial roof to free rain and snow.

How can one remember thirst?

Life-giving 氣 cycles through the Marker mandala, earth the condition of our thirst. Thirst an unseen force opposed to inertia, its vector vertical skyward to the sun.

Death stayed distant from me until the summer after high-school graduation. My friend Terrie went on a six-mile run with her college soccer team, her freshman year hadn't yet begun, she collapsed under the sun. Help arrived too late. Her body shut down and she entered a coma state. I drove up to the hospital from San Diego to Irvine with two other friends, but she had already gone—cause of death, dehydration and heatstroke. Hospital blur mausoleum; no memory of the drive home. The physicality of thirst, its physiological, biochemical process: heart rate elevates, body temperature elevates, cells swell, blood pressure drops, plasma volume drops, vision dims, delirium, seizures, hypovolemic shock, hallucinations, cells burst, organs bleed, coma, death. Thirst exists between the literal and the figurative, the biological and the metaphysical, matter and spirit—it is one gate between life and death, defined by a cellular need.

What dwells in the many cells of the soul? A spirit that thirsts? What we know, no doubt: souls never leave us.

"Blank the crack and mark no language or predator camera can recover," writes Susan Howe in her essay on Chris Marker.

Senior year Terrie was voted class president. I had known her since elementary school, Cathedral of the Valley. Her parents' faith assured them that their daughter's soul had ascended to heaven. This knowledge, however, didn't come with any appearance of solace, closure, or acceptance. What her older brother believed was a mystery to me. He seemed lost at sea, her parents, shipwrecked. Belief taught us that to be marked by God could mean early death (Cain notwithstanding). Her death left us with the perils of thirst in the fact of her absence.

. . . and now adrift and lost / Riding an ocean of a million waves / We die of thirst.

This Iphis thinks to herself before her wedding to golden-haired Ianthe. Or in another translation of Ovid's retelling: *I shall thirst in the midst of the waters.* Age thirteen and no one knew Iphis was a girl save her mother, Telethusa, and her nurse. Her father, blind Ligdus, had arranged her marriage to Ianthe. When Telethusa was pregnant with Iphis, Ligdus had asked that the baby be put to death if it were a girl. Telethusa, distraught, had a dream where she was visited by the goddess Io/Isis—crescent horns, royal robe, halo of golden wheat—who tells her to forget her husband's words and have her baby, boy or girl. Iphis was born, raised as a boy. She was schoolmates with Ianthe, both became wounded by love for one another. But her wedding day nears and Iphis despairs, for she desires what Nature will not allow, her ardor no less true than Ianthe's. *I shall thirst in the midst of the waters. Mediis sitiemus in undis*: Ovid's line falls mid-story, in the middle of the waves, the waters, at the peak of her passion, at the realization that what is so near at hand, her love to be, can never be. Desperate, Telethusa embraces the altar of Isis, tears the ribbons from her daughter's hair, and prays for help. The temple trembles, the doors swing open, the crescent horns shine like the moon, sistras shake. As they walk from the temple, Iphis's stride starts to lengthen, her complexion darkens, her hair shortens, her strength and energy increase, and she "steps into manhood." The wedding fires burn.

Kuafu is also consumed by passion, of a different nature. His myth, more than 2,500 years old, is immortalized by a four-character proverb: 夸父追日 (*Kuafu zhui ri*), "Kuafu chases the sun."

The myth of Kuafu's first appearance in the written record can be found in the 山海經 (*Shan Hai Jing*), or *The Classic of Mountains and Seas*, an encyclopedic geography/ethnography/cosmography compiled sometime during the fourth and first centuries BC. It is seen as a Chinese primer of mythology, as well as the world's first travelogue and first bestiary, not necessarily of imaginative creatures but of what was recorded to be real. Traditionally thought to have been divinely transmitted, the text is divided into three, or five, sections of eighteen books; the first section of five books maps the five zones of mountains (southern, northern, eastern, western, and central) and is further divided into twenty-six chapters, or guideways. The rest of the *Classic* charts the world beyond the seas, within the seas, and through the great wilderness.

According to the *Shan Hai Jing* heaven is a round canopy composed of nine layers that covers a square earth. The five mountain zones support the sky, and the four corners of the earth are surrounded by four seas scattered with islands. Surrounding the four seas is the great wilderness, while the four extremities, or four poles, mark the edges of the known world. The five colors bluegreen, red, white, black, and yellow, and certain magic numbers like three, four, five, and nine, also figure into its cosmology. Over the centuries the book has been copied and recopied, edited and reedited, as well as illustrated and annotated with extensive commentaries. The oldest extant copy is a Song Dynasty edition of 1180 AD edited by Yu Mao. Of

China's long history of manuscript culture, Xiaofei Tian writes: "Just underneath the smooth, fixed surface of a modern printed edition is a chaotic and unstable world." Richard Strassberg's introduction to his annotated edition of the *Shan Hai Jing* traces some of the "destabilizing linguistic, textual, historical, and cultural factors" involved in the many incarnations of this book, which has been translated into several Indo-European languages—with at least two complete translations and three partial translations published in English—as well as multiple translations into Japanese and *bai hua*, vernacular Chinese.

The radiating details one can pursue along the various threads of the *Classic*, whether historical, alchemical, philological, pharmaceutical, sacral, and so on, are as vast as the seas. It is an *Odyssey* without the plotline. Within the book one finds observations and stories of deities and demigods, goddesses, winged fish, trees, plants, minerals, rivers, sacrificial rituals, rivers, medical prescriptions, tribes, a tiger with nine human heads, divine genealogies, dragons, rhinoceros, the Land the People with Perforated Chests, the Land of the Great Moon Tribe, an ox-like beast with an aura as brilliant as the sun and moon—it is a book of folklore, book of beasts, book of myths and beliefs, book of magic, book of minerals and plants, and on and on. Tides, we're told, are caused by a sea serpent coming and going into its cave; certain mountains and a particular tree serve as ladders to heaven, objects akin to the carved Y-shaped ladders of the Dogons of West Africa that lead to the ancestors. The origins of this text, as Lu Xun and other scholars have postulated, are shamanistic in nature, and specifically rooted in a certain *wu*-shaman culture of female priests who served as a bridge between humans and the gods, these shamans "skilled in herbal medicine, divination, dream interpretation, exorcism, omenology, genealogy, calendrical and astronomical calculation, sacrifices, sacred performances, rainmaking, as well as certain rites of resurrection," as Strassberg notes. The *wu*-shamans play an important role in the *Shan Hai Jing* and are keepers of the secrets of immortality.

The British oracle bone specialist L. C. Hopkins, brother of the poet Gerard Manley Hopkins, describes how the Chinese characters for *wu* (巫), "shaman or witch," and *wu* (舞), "to dance," both originate from the same oracle-bone forms that depict a dancing thaumaturgic shaman holding plumes or other ritual objects in her hands. Strassberg tells us that a first-century dictionary glossed *wu* (巫) as *zhu* (祝), or "priest-invocator," as well as saying it derived from the homophonic character "to dance," which illustrates the fluttering sleeves of female shamans as they danced to invoke the gods. Figure 1, a detail from a zither excavated from a circa fourth century BC tomb in present-day Henan province, shows the painted image of a *wu*-shaman holding a snake in each hand. What is strange and supernatural to us is merely a part of the everyday as portrayed in the *Shan Hai Jing* ("Things possessing anomalous forms are those born with divine nature"), and so the compilation of a guide, a book of rites, a book of medicine, a book of tribes. In *The Master Who Embraces Simplicity*, the fourth-century Daoist Ge Hong writes, "All mountains, whether large or small, contain gods and powers, and the strength of these divinities is directly proportional to the size of the mountains. To enter the mountains without the proper rites and preparations is to be certain of anxiety or harm." Today, an English translation of *The Classic of Mountains and Seas* reads like a fantastical contemporary prose-poem, in its structural and textual repetitions, its absence of narrative continuity, its fragmented cohesiveness, its lightning turns of image and place. As Anne Birrell writes in her translated edition:

> It is a marked feature of classical Chinese mythology that myths are narrated in a lapidary, exiguous style. In general, they constitute a collection of fragments, rather than extended narrative. In this fragmented, minimalist expression, it is possible to conjecture that they appear as early Greek myth once did, before Homer and Hesiod, and later, for Roman myth, Ovid rewrote the ancient mythology,

systematizing, standardizing, and homogenizing a once vibrantly discordant set of traditions. In the *Classic*, mythic strands that belong to a single figure are scattered untidily through the eighteen books.

Figure 1

The Jin Dynasty poet Tao Yuanming (Tao Qian, 365?–427 AD)—adopted by the Song Dynasty poet Su Shi six hundred years later as his poet-hero: "How could it be his poetry alone that I love? His person, too, has moved me"—wrote a series of thirteen poems called "On Reading *The Classic of Mountains and Seas*." In her book *Tao Yuanming & Manuscript Culture*, Xiaofei Tian says this poem cycle is unique in Chinese literary history for being the first ever written on the topic of reading, where "the reading experience is explicitly embedded in the poems." It is well known in classical Chinese poetry circles that Tao Qian reinvented the poetic genre of *youxian* (the poetry of roaming, transcendent immortals) so that the immortal experience included reading, contemplation, and drinking. The opening poem of his poem cycle establishes the setting and occasion of the reading of the *Classic*, as seen here in this excerpt of David Hinton's translation:

It's early summer. Everything's lush.
Our house set deep among broad trees,
birds delight in taking refuge here.
I too love this little place. And now
the plowing and planting are finished,
I can return to my books again and read.
[…]   My eyes
wander *Tales of Emp–eror Mu*, float along
on *Mountains and Seas* pictures….
Look around. All time and space within
sight—if not here, where will joy come?

I recall reading the last lines of *The Iliad* on the final stretch of the
A Train to Rockaway Beach where the rail line suddenly divides the
water and seems to hover just above a sunlight-rippling Jamaica Bay.
Hector the peacemaker, tamer of horses, laid upon the funeral pyre.
Dawn the next day, the eleventh day, wine poured on the fire, his
white bones wrapped in purple cloth and placed in a golden urn, then
buried under a mound of earth and stones … and on to the feast and
celebration. All time and space within sight of the Bay, the rumbling
of the train, sun-phase.

I wrote a series of five poems in an abecedarian bestiarium that
were also inspired by reading the *Shan Hai Jing* as well as Tao Qian's
poems "On Reading." One of them is titled "Yingshao" and goes:

Follow the third guideway thru
the Western Mountains to reach
Scholartree River Peak covered
with green realgar, cinnabar, Lang-
gan Stone, yellow gold, silver, and jade.
There you'll find the Supreme Deity's
Garden of Peace, tended by Yingshao

who has the body of a horse, a human
face, tiger's stripes, and bird's wings.
His home is the Four Seas he
circles thru, while making sounds
"like reading books aloud."
Of the unknown
heed Daoist Ge Hong:
Never enter a mountain lightly.

The story of Kuafu first appears in book eight of the *Classic*, in the guideway to the northern regions beyond the seas. Here is Strassberg's translation of the story with Jiang Yinghao's corresponding late sixteenth-century illustration of Kuafu (Figure 2a) as well as Cheng Huoyin's 1855 rendition (Figure 2b):

Kuafu the Boaster chased after the sun and ran to where it sets. He
became thirsty and wanted to drink, so he drank from the Yellow
River and the Wei River. The water from the Yellow River and the
Wei River was not sufficient for him so he went north to drink from
the Grand Lake. But before he reached it, he died of thirst on the
road. He threw down his staff, which became transformed into the
Deng Forest.

Figure 2a

Figure 2b

The story of Kuafu also appears in book seventeen of the *Shan Hai Jing*, the guideway to the great wilderness in the north. Here is Birrell's translation of the story, where Kuafu is Boast Father:

> In the middle of the Great Wilderness there is a mountain. Its name Mount Successcity-carriesthesky. There is someone on this mountain. His ear ornaments are two yellow snakes, and he is holding two yellow snakes. His name is Boast Father. Sovereign Earth gave birth to Faith. Faith gave birth to Boast Father. Boast Father's strength knew no bounds. He longed to race against the light of the sun. He caught up with it at Ape Valley. He scooped some water from the great River to drink, but it wasn't enough. He ran towards Big Marsh, but just before he reached it, he died here by this mountain. Responding Dragon had already killed Jest Much, and now he also killed Boast Father. Then Responding Dragon left for the southern region and settled there. That is why there is so much rain in the southern region. Besides these places, there is the country of Nogut, whose people have Laden as their family name.

Book fourteen, the guideway to the great wilderness in the east, says that Yinglong (Responding/Winged Dragon), dwells at the southern pole of a mountain, and after killing both Chiyou (Jest Much, cousin of Jes Grew) and Kuafu, he couldn't return to his mountain, and so the earth became plagued with droughts—thus people constructed an image of Yinglong to make it rain. The fourth century BC text *The Questions of Heaven* notes that Yinglong aided Yu the Great in taming the waters during an epic flood during the third millennium BC. Yu the Great, mythical author of the *Shan Hai Jing* and legendary founder of the Xia Dynasty, united the land into nine provinces and forged nine bronze *ding* vessels, one for each province, cast with images of the marvelous creatures from each province. Figure 3 is Jiang's illustration of Yinglong. The second telling of the myth is both truncated and extended compared to the first, most noticeably marked by the absence of the Deng Forest, and by Kuafu's double death: first from internal thirst, and then he is killed by the dragon that embodies thirst.

Figure 3

Kuafu's name can mean either "the boaster" or "the praised." It can also mean "giant." In the passage that follows the Kuafu story in book eight, the country of Kuafu is thought to be the same as the country of Bofu, populated by giants. Here, Kuafu holds a green snake in his right hand and a yellow snake in his left and to the east of where the giants live are two trees called Deng Forest. Figure 4a shows Jiang Yinghao's illustration of Kuafu/Bofu and the two trees above him; Figure 4b, from an encyclopedia published in 1725, and Figure 4c, from Cheng Huoyin's 1855 edition, also show Kuafu in this country of giants. In book three's second guideway through the northern mountains, a bird with four wings, one eye, and a dog's tail called 嚣 (*xiao*: raucous, clamor, contempt) is said to be another manifestation of Kuafu. The bird makes a sound like a magpie, and eating it cures abdominal pain and indigestion. Figure 5 is Jiang's illustration of Raucous-Bird.

Figure 4a

Figure 4b

Figure 4c   Figure 5

The third-century poet Guo Pu, who was mythologized as a Daoist Immortal after his execution, wrote one of the most famous commentaries on the *Shan Hai Jing* (the edition with Jiang's illustrations retain Guo Pu's commentary) as well as three hundred six-line poems of four graphs per line called *Encomiums to the Illustrations of the Classic of Mountains and Seas*. He said the *Classic* was filled with "universal knowledge." In book three's third guideway through the western mountains, a creature called Jufu, or Lifter, is described as resembling a Yu-Ape with leopard and tiger markings on its arms and is adept at throwing things. Guo Pu comments that Jufu is also called Kuafu in a different version of the *Shan Hai Jing*. Figure 6 depicts this image of Kuafu as Jufu. In book five's sixth guideway through the central mountains, there is a Mount Kuafu with palm and wild plum trees, arrow-bamboo, buffalo, antelope, golden pheasant, large deposits of jade and iron, and wild horses. To the north of this mountain a grove of peach trees grow that some believe is the Deng Forest Kuafu transformed into.

Figure 6

Mortal, god, giant, bird, dragon, ape—Kuafu's shifting physical form complements the cosmology of the five phases that figure in the myth. Kuafu the Boaster (or the Praised) is the grandson of Sovereign Earth (the male/female deity Houtu) and is thus associated with earth and the color yellow; he competes with fire (sun, also symbolized by the legendary Flame Emperor who appears in the *Classic*) and is overcome by water (thirst/Yellow and Wei Rivers/Grand Lake/ Big Marsh/Responding Dragon), eventually transforming into wood (Deng Forest/grove of peach trees). The element iron within the mountain can be seen (unseen) as the metal of transformation.

Liezi, the attributed author of *Liezi*, one of the three primary texts of Daoism, lived sometime around the sixth or fourth centuries BC and traveled by riding the wind. It is possible that his book wasn't compiled until the fourth century AD. Liezi says, "I enter the vortex with the inflow and leave with the outflow, follow the Way of the water instead of imposing a course of my own; this is how I tread it." In the chapter titled "The Questions of Tang" (referring to the Sage-King Tang who founded the Yin, or Shang, Dynasty in the second millennium BC), the story of Kuafu is recounted, here in A. C. Graham's translation:

> K'ua-fu, rating his strength too high, wanted to chase the daylight, and pursued it to the brink of the Yü valley. He was thirsty and wished to drink, and hurried to drink the Yellow River and the Wei. The Yellow River and the Wei did not quench his thirst, and he ran North intending to drink the Great Marsh, but died of thirst on the road before he reached it. The staff which dropped soaked up the fat and flesh of his corpse and grew into Teng forest. Teng forest spread until it covered several thousand miles.

Unlike the other tellings, Liezi emphasizes Kuafu's negative motivation ("rating his strength too high"), and also attributes the transformation of Kuafu's physical body (and not his staff) from flesh into widespread forest.

Tao Qian also retells the Kuafu story in the ninth poem of his "On Reading *The Classic of Mountains and Seas*." Here is the whole of the poem I've translated:

> Kuafu's foolish ambition   was so great
> to face the sun in a race   They
> reached the Yu Gorge together
> neither victorious   neither defeated
> With extraordinary divine power   the god
> drained the river   but how could he ever
> overrun Sun?   Where his body perished
> Deng Forest remained   merit attained

Tao Qian turns the tale into a deeper allegory of transformation where Kuafu's measure of thirst is implied to be too great to satiate. It isn't the sun that defeats him but his own capacity for thirst. And even then he is not defeated: he may not be able to enjoy the fruits (peaches) of his achievement but others after him will. Unlike Kuafu, "man," the fool in Beaumarchais's *Le Mariage de Figaro* observes, "is the animal who drinks without thirst and is lustful year-round," a quote the twentieth-century scholar-novelist Qian Zhongshu quotes in an essay on prejudice. In this case, to be more than man is to thirst.

The figure of Kuafu has survived through songs, poems, paintings, stories, novels, cartoons, operas. The *Handbook of Chinese Mythology*, published in 2005, tells us that in Lingbao County in Henan Province many aspects of the landscape have been named after Kuafu, including a Kuafu Mountain where a Qing Dynasty tablet was discovered with his tale carved in it, and a Kuafu Valley where offerings are still made to him. Kuafu appears on a 1987 twenty-*fen* stamp designed by Lou Jiaben; many sculptures have been made of him, including one displayed at the Qingdao Olympic Theme Park that opened in 2008. In Shu-min Lin's thirty-eight-foot-long art installation of the Kuafu myth, one follows a beam of light as it illuminates holographic images of male nudes merging into one another. The priciest reincarnation of Kuafu must be the current KuaFu Space Project, a government research initiative to build three spacecrafts—KuaFu-A and KuaFu-B1 and -B2—that will study the weather and the sun: projected launch date 2015/2016, though now apparently suspended indefinitely. The Kuafu myth has been integrated into the apex of nationalism and interstellar science. Official and consumerist propaganda popularly promote Kuafu as an icon of the struggle for technological innovation and surmounting nature. A modern version of the myth has Kuafu chasing the sun in order to stop it from crashing into Earth.

In his 1937 talk "On Contradictions," Chairman Mao criticized Kuafu and mythology in general, saying the "subjectively conceived" transformation of contradictions in myths lack a "concrete identity" and only have an "imaginary identity." Such "imaginary identities" Mao linked to metaphysics, which he defines in Marxist-Leninist lingo as "reactionary idealism" that "looks outside a thing for its causes of development" against the ever-changing movement of contradictions he so championed as materialist dialectics. His argument, intended to eradicate dogmatic thinking in the Party, seems at best displaced and oversimplified. Tracing the many manifestations of Kuafu, for one, it is obvious that myth dialectically translates between places, times, circumstances, languages, in concrete ways, intertwined as they are with the conditions of the real. They are, indeed, *bundles of relation*, and as real as words. They arise out of the real as they transform it from within. They are the fabric of dreams, lend science a language, hold the keys to our thirst, emerge from our deepest collective fears and desires, while also serve as models for our own beliefs, relationships, and realities. Even the younger Mao wrote his own mythology in a much different way than he would later in life: "To establish and build the Communist Party is in fact to prepare the conditions for the elimination of the Communist Party and all political parties." How many politicians continue to work for the hope of their own power becoming obsolete? Passion is thirst.

Guan Zhong, prime minister to the Duke of Huan in the seventh century BC and the forerunner of the Legalists who so enamored Elias Canetti, determined that the source of all political and social problems came down to one issue: water. He says, "Therefore the sage's transformation of the world arises from solving the problem of water. If water is united, the human heart will be corrected. If water is pure and clean the heart of the people will readily be unified and desirous of cleanliness. If the people's heart is changed their conduct will not be depraved. So the sage's government does not consist of talking to people and persuading them family by family. The pivot of a sage's work is water."

With water as pivot, *as we drink / we hear thirst / slaked*, to translate. For a new line.

"The poem is the answer's absence," Maurice Blanchot writes. Returning to the original question posed by Marker's *wu xing* mandala-frame, stilled then swept away by the passing of subsequent frames per second, I offer Kuafu as one reply—memory rewritten in myth, myth rewritten in poetry, through time and translation, in an ongoing passage of remembrance. The boat moves as she looks away from the camera toward the sunlight sea silence 氣. Kuafu, ears full of snakes, is an evolving contradiction. Snakes, holy guardians of the grave, dwellers underground, of water and air. The four-character saying mentioned earlier, 夸父追日—"Kuafu chases the sun"—contains a double meaning: either as a negative cognitive metaphor for one who overestimates his own abilities and, godlike, blindly acts without thought of the consequences to his own ruin, or as a positive cognitive metaphor for one whose passion and perseverance is so great, sramana-like, even if thirst should overcome him, his aspiration will realize a certain good. Chasing the light. Chasing the flame. Less Icarus than Faust to us. From some inner responding dragon of *-ters.

One sees a circle of light until one realizes it is actually a point of fire.

 . . . je reste comme ça plus soif la langue rentre la bouche se referme. . .

The tenth-century geographer Al-Masu'di said that the writings of his predecessor al-Jahiz "polish rust from the mind." He noted that al-Jahiz listed a certain kind of crane-like bird as one of the three most marvelous things he had ever witnessed in the world. This bird was called Malik al-Hazin—"Master of Sadness"—a type of heron. Malik al-Hazin, observed al-Jahiz, always stands on the edge of tidal flats to watch the water recede. She is afraid the water might disappear from the surface of the earth and she would then die of thirst.

✣

And thirst. What I remember is thirst—below, in the depths, in the well—and that I drank from it.

—Alejandra Pizarnik, translated by Yvette Siegert

Maxim Amelin is a poet, critic, editor, and translator who received the 2013 Solzhenitsyn Prize for his contributions to Russian literature. The author of three books of poetry and a collection of prose and poems, Bent Speech *(2011), he is the editor-in-chief at OGI publishing.*

Классическая ода
В. В. Маяковскому

Зам. председателя Земшара!
вознаграждён за гертруды,
ходи по лезвию пожара
и битому стеклу воды
свободно, без препон и пошлин,
иль стой на площади, опошлен,
в потёках жертвенной мочи,—
лишь в сумрачное время суток
кучкующихся проституток,
смотри, В. В., не потопчи.

Смотри, в слепящее рекламой
многоочитое табло
неосторожно, самый-самый!
ножищей в тысячу кило
не звездани, В. В., навылет,
а то напополам распилят
и переплавят на металл.—
Ломая молниями строчки,

Classical Ode to
V. V. Mayakovsky

Vice-Chairman of the Globosphere!
Your hero-works will long abide;
though oft you've walked the flame's bright edge
and paced the shattered water's tide,
it's time to shed impediments
and stand atop your pediment,
which shines with streams of sacrificial
urine. As usual, when dusk grows deep,
the hookers cluster at your feet.
Look here, V. V., they can't be trampled.

And look! Billboards and blinding rows
of flashing screens—those can't be trashed!
You'll have to stow your two-ton switchblade
when you go walking, for if you slash
one ad they'll saw you through the middle
and smelt you down for cheap scrap metal.
So don't screw up those monstrous posters.
Who dreamed of lines in laddered steps

о свежестиранной сорочке
и памятнике кто мечтал?

Ты, друг всего и вся на свете
и лучший враг всего и вся,
из тех апартаментов в эти
переливающегося,
ты, для горилл и павианов,
как вывернутый Жорж Иванов
для павианов и горилл,
поверивших, что солнце—люстра,
но, слава Богу, Заратустра
так никогда не говорил.

В четырехстопном ямбе трудно
сложить сочувственную речь
тебе, как тонущее судно
от гибели предостеречь,—
ни славы нет, ни силы класса,
ни рябчика, ни ананаса...
Стань, кем ты не был, кем ты был,
останься,—старцем и подростком,
всех шумных улиц перекрестком
и жеребцом для всех кобыл!

and craved respect from lowest plebs
while always wearing laundered collars?

It's you, best friend of all creation,
and foremost fiend of all, or many;
you had no fixed accommodation,
maneuvering 'mid folks aplenty;
antithesis of that artiste—
himself no friend to apes or beasts
who think a lampshade is the sun—
the émigré, Georges Ivanov;
and thank the Lord you are both one-offs,
not Zarathustra's Overman.

It's difficult composing paeans
to you in four-beat lines of iambs,
just as it's hard to right the ship
of love that's so hell-bent to wreck.
The working class is one big louse;
there's no more pineapples, no grouse.
Become the man you never were:
grow old, but stay tradition's scourge,
the crossroads where all streets converge,
the stallion mounting every mare!

Олегу Чухонцеву

Зверь огнедышащий с пышною гривой,
серпокогтистый, твой норов игривый
      не понаслышке знаком
всем, кто, вдыхая гниения запах,
некогда мызган в чешуйчатых лапах,
      лизан стальным языком,

дважды раздвоенным, всем, кто копытом
бит по зубам и пером ядовитым
      колот и глажен не раз
больно и нежно, кто чувствовал близко
испепеляющего Василиска
      взгляд немигающих глаз,

взгляд на себе.—Никаких предисловий,
лишь заохотится мяса и крови,
      зев отверзается твой
и наполняется плотью утроба
плотно с причмоком,—навыкате оба
      только не сыты жратвой

ока; бывает: ни рылом ни ухом
не поведет, расстилается пухом,

for Oleg Chukhontsev

Fire-breathing beast, fumes wreathing your figure,
with sickle-claws clenched your playful nature
      is clear: an open book
read by all who've caught the whiff of ruin
as they're clamped in those glittering talons,
      the skin on their backs

raked by your steel-file tongue; or who've taken
hooves in the teeth, been stabbed with a poison
      pen; or who've realized
(too late) that they're in too deep; or whose gaze
has met the basilisk's, his deadly rays
      loosed from unblinking eyes.

Eyes were all they saw. You gave no prelude,
cutting right to the kill, feasting on blood.
      Your gruesome maw opens—
you glut your fetid gut, you slake your dry
gullet, slurping, smacking, rolling your eyes
      in satisfaction

with your meal and something more ... though fodder
is what I have plainly watched you offer—

кротко виляя хвостом.—
О Государство! не ты ли?—Повадки,
взлет ли стремя, пребывая ль в упадке,
те же, что в изверге том,—

разницы нет никакой. Поневоле
тыщами слизью набитых: «Доколе!»—
во всеуслышанье ртов
жертвы б во чреве твоем провещали.
(—*Если тебе не хватает печали,*
я поделиться готов.)

not slaughter—to the lambs.
O State! Is this you? Whether you're planing
new heights or wallowing in your waning,
       that leviathan

and you share these traits. Thousands of victims
would cry "Enough!" from your belly's cistern,
       their voices thick and phlegm-
filled for all who've ears to hear. They have to.
(*I bear these woes and more. If you've too few,*
       I'll gladly share them.)

Born in Madrid, Medardo Fraile (1925–2013) was a short-story writer in the mode of Anton Chekhov or Katherine Mansfield and, like them, was a chronicler of the minor tragedies and triumphs of ordinary life. His stories first appeared in English in 2014 with Things Look Different in the Light.

En vilo

Pascualín Porres vino al mundo, llegó a 1,60 de estatura y creyó, hasta su muerte, que estaba entre personas. Como en el medio en que vivió la única persona era él, le utilizaron todos los días, de forma que Pascualín tuvo siempre trabajo, nunca dinero, usó corbata, tuvo mocasines, gemelos, sombrerito, pañuelos finos y agua de colonia. Nunca logró ir del todo bien vestido, ni del todo limpio; nunca paralizó billetes grandes ni fue más lejos de Logroño. No se casó. Paseó con amiguitas, pero no riñó con ninguna lo bastante para fundar un hogar. Se enfurruñaba con ellas, dos, tres veces, y no volvía. Muchos se habían casado en las condiciones de él, pero dando a los demás la lata: el banco adelantaba lo del piso, el padrino pagaba la iglesia, el viaje a Mallorca el sindicato, el traje de la novia la madrina, los suegros el comedor, los amigos la cama, los conocidos la batería de cocina y aún quedaban en reserva parientes para pagar la cuna y el tocólogo. Demasiado impudor, descaro penoso—pensaba Pascualín—para acostarse con una mujer, aunque fuera para toda la vida, que era—decían—la forma de acostarse menos. Había que aguantarse y dormir solo. Lo contrario era forzar el débito conyugal, rugir como una fiera sobre cabezas humanas. Pascualín Porres no rebuznó como el asno, ni se llevó la gallina como la zorra, ni acaparó . . .

Treading Lightly

Pascualín Porres came into the world, grew to be five foot two and a half, and believed, right up until his death, that he was living among real people. Since, in the circles in which he moved, he was the only real person, the others made use of him every day, which meant that Pascualín always had work, but no money, wore a tie and moccasins, cuff links, a hat, fancy handkerchiefs, and eau de cologne, but never somehow succeeded in being smartly dressed or entirely clean; he never managed to hang on to any large banknotes nor did he ever travel any further than Logroño. He never married. He had a few girlfriends, but never quarreled with any of them seriously enough to set up home with one of them. He fell out with them once, twice, three times, then never came back. Many men in his situation had married, but always at the expense of others: the bank loaned the money for the apartment, the godfather paid for the church, the trade union for the trip to Mallorca, the godmother for the bridal gown, the in-laws the dining-room furniture, some friends the bed, certain acquaintances the kitchen equipment, and there were still a few relatives left to pay for the crib and the obstetrician. What shamelessness, what barefaced cheek—thought Pascualín—and all in order to be able to sleep with a woman, even if it was for the rest of your life, which was—they said—the surest way of *not* getting to sleep with a woman. Far better to accept one's lot and sleep alone. The alternative meant demanding one's conjugal rights and being more beast than man. Pascualín Porres did not bray like the donkey, or run off with a chicken like the fox, or steal jewels like the magpie, or kill lambs like the wolf, nor did he laugh cruelly like the hyena, and he never had to flee like the hare, nor did he wake anyone up like the cockerel, or clown around like the monkey, nor, like the bear, did he tear out someone's throat, all the while looking as nice as pie. He did his best every day not to strike a discordant note in a world of people who had written books about their history and their philosophy. A world that had learned painfully and slowly to use toilet paper, to wear glasses, to starch collars, to adorn itself with ribbons, to cut and coif its hair, to distinguish between a quince and an apple, to legislate for injustice, to casually come out with such words and phrases as *really, nevertheless, therefore, never mind, we must take into account . . .* Pascualín Porres always spontaneously gave his heart, like a fruit that was there for everyone, like something that did not altogether belong to him, just as a bird's heart does not entirely belong to it. And he trod very lightly through life, putting down little roots here and there, gentle, tickling roots, incapable of causing a crack in a wall or of scratching anyone. Slender roots like a small brush for painting on moustaches, innocent, fresh, the kind a careless earthworm could easily bite through. Pascualín Porres always asked others if they agreed with his tastes, his attitudes, his ideas, his words. When he caught the flu and someone came to visit him, he would breathe more quietly, turn to face the wall whenever he sneezed or coughed, and urge his visitor not to linger, not to risk infection, not to waste any time on his account. On the bus, he always went straight to the back so as not to get in the way of the passengers behind. The few modestly bound books he owned had been read by everyone and they diminished in number by the day. The little money he earned was available to all, even if this meant him spending the rest of the month at home, kicking his heels. Pascualín had only two major vices: movies, which made him feel as quixotic as Gary Cooper, as bold as Burt Lancaster, as elegantly shy as Anthony Perkins, as charming as David Niven, as wild as James Dean, as sexually ambivalent as Elvis Presley. Movies and the windows—but *only* the windows—of bookstores and stationers. A bone-handled penknife, a box of coloring pencils, a finely produced encyclopedia or story, a rosary of rose petals, a book with a smart jacket, all these, for reasons unknown, fascinated him. He planned his purchases, but never bought anything. When talking, Pascualín would rely on such phrases as: "I thought that ... but, of course, if you don't like the idea ... "; "Listen, would you mind ... ?"; "No, you go first ... "; "Do you like this sort of suit?"; "Do you think we should ... ?"; "Don't worry, I have change ... "; "What I meant to say was ... "; "Sorry, I got delayed ... "; "If you don't want to, you just have to say ... " He was constantly correcting himself, always quite willingly, even if it embarrassed him, even if he thought he was right, because he didn't want to be a nuisance, to hurt anyone; on the contrary, he wanted to tread lightly, to tiptoe delicately through this world of roses, this great civilized world full of people.

However, all his colleagues, friends, and relatives, the people who had, at first, offered him their opinions—all the while viewing him, of course, as utterly absurd—began deliberately leading him astray in order to make a fool of him. They convinced him to wear green ties with navy-blue jackets, they would arrange to meet him early in the morning, then stand him up, they caused him to miss some really good movies, they vanished whenever he asked a favor, they gossiped about him and mocked him behind his back when he persisted in his humanly impossible desire to have them speak to him gently, to acknowledge his generosity, his selflessness, for at least one of them to be what he thought they all were: a proper person.

In his last few years, Pascualín Porres's dream faded. Contrary to what his heart thought or his head felt, the will-o'-the-wisps of their mockery assailed him all too frequently, whenever, which was always, he would have preferred not to see them. He died young, because he knew that long visits can become tiresome, that one should not outstay one's welcome. His sojourn among the living lasted only as long as was proper. Before he died, he glanced shyly around at the few familiar faces in his room. He said: "Please, if you notice that I'm dying, do tell me." The others looked at each other, thinking: "He doesn't change. He's as big an idiot as ever." And they said nothing, because this time it seemed wrong to reveal to him what the doctor had said or, on the contrary, to lie. Poor Pascualín Porres! What would he do if they did tell him? Would he close his own eyes so as not to bother them? Would he fold his own sensitive, dying hands? Or don his own shroud? Douse himself in eau de cologne? Neatly align his legs? When they had such a good time doing it for him afterward!

The hearse, with Pascualín inside, drove, swift and unnoticed, past the cinema he usually attended, past the new window display at the stationer's where Pascualín had so often paused. Now, had he been able to, he would have seen a book whose spine said almost in a murmur: "The vampire's strength lies in the fact that no one believes in his existence."

Aigerim Tazhi, born in the Kazakhstani city of Aktobe, is the author of a book of poetry and has received numerous literary prizes in Kazakhstan and Russia. In 2011 she was a finalist for the Russian Debut Prize in poetry.

На ладан не дыши—дышать здесь нечем.
Зря говорят, что сельский воздух лечит.
Саднящий в носоглотке дым костра
меняет очертания. Вглядись же.
Буреют в куче скошенные астры.
Садовник выкорчевывает липу,
которая ни разу не цвела.

Don't take a last breath—nothing to breathe here.
In vain they say that country air cures.
The campfire smoke burns your nostrils.
it alters all outlines. Look closely.
Cut asters wilt in heaps.
A gardener uproots a linden
that never bloomed, not once.

Волнистые белые линии
на голубой воде.
Облако? Лебедь? Лилия?
Руки тяни. Задел
за что-то пушистое, крощечное,
Отдернул ладонь. Держу
хорошенького ангелочка
за порванный парашют.

Wavy white lines
on light blue water.
A cloud? A swan? A lily?
I stretch out my hands. Brushed
against something fluffy, tiny,
Drew back a palm. I hold
onto the ripped parachute
of a cute little cherub.

ветер в комнате. дождь
по эту сторону подоконника

на поверхности пола
водная блажь и травинка
тоненькая

девушка засыпает с библией
просыпается с сонником

она бы давно выздоровела
но стоит на учете хроником

wind in the room. rain
on this side of the windowsill

on the surface of the floor
a watery caprice and a very thin
blade of grass

a girl falls asleep with a bible
wakes up with a dream-book

she might have recovered long ago
but is in the books as incurable

Заполняя расписание оставшейся жизни,
рассчитываю на реинкарнаию.
Земля—временное пристанище.
Гроб семечком высеивается, закапывается.
Лопается червями червонное вздутие.
Холм отпочковывается от почвы.
Оградой заявка на суверенитет.
Подсолнух пьет соки подземные мертвые,
всасывая краски из мраморного портрета
вместо.
У меня по плану стоять под облаком
стволом, не телом,
шалеть от солнца, маслом лосниться,
время от времени заклеванной зрелостью
подкармливать похотливых птиц.

Fulfilling a program for the rest of life,
I count on reincarnation.
Earth is a temporary shelter.
A coffin is sown, planted like a seed.
A crimson bloating bursts with worms.
A hill swells from the soil.
A fence as an application for sovereignty.
A sunflower drinks subterranean juices of the dead
absorbing paint from a marble portrait
instead.
I have a plan to stand under a cloud
as a trunk, not a body,
to go crazy from the sun, shine with oil,
from time to time be pecked at in my ripeness
to fatten lascivious birds

Born in Beirut in 1972, Rabee Jaber is one of the Arab world's most widely acclaimed
authors. He has written eighteen novels to date, in which he explores Lebanon's past from
a host of angles, ranging from historical to fantastical fiction.

الاعترافات

«أبي كان يخطف الناس ويقتلهم. أخي يقول إنه رأى أبي يتحول في الحرب
من شخص يعرفه الى شخص لا يعرفه. هذا أخي الكبير. أخي الصغير لم
أعرفه، أعرف صورته، أعرف وجهه، يشبهني في الصور ـ كان يشبهني ـ أكثر
مما يشبه أخي الكبير. أسميه أخي الصغير وكنا كلنا في البيت نسميه ـ في
رؤوسنا نسميه، وحتى من دون أن نذكره ونحن نحكي، كانت صوره تملأ البيت ـ
ماذا كنت أقول؟ أسميه أخي الصغير ولم يكن أخي الصغير ولكنه الصغير لأنه
ظل صغيرا، لأنه لم يكبر، لأنهم قتلوه وهو صغير.

كم مرة رأيت أخواتي ساكتات في الصالون (كان الصالون غرفة البيت
الآمنة والملجأ ساعة القصف) كأنهن في جنازة، يتوزعن على الكنبة الطويلة
ذات الغطاء المخمل الزيتي، ينظرن إلى صوره المكبرة على الحائط، وعلى زاوية
الصورة الشريط الأسود؟ كم مرة رأيت أختي الكبيرة تلتفت دامعة وتنظر إليّ
أدخل حاملا سندويشة ـ كل الوقت آكل سندويشات يروق القصف عند الغروب
فتركض أمي إلى المطبخ؛ تنبه عليّ ألا ألحقها إلى المطبخ لكنني ألحقها؛ أمي
تلف سندويشات مرتديلا وخيار وأنا آكلها ـ أذكر أختي الآن كأن هذه السنوات
كلها لم تمر، مرت ولم تمر، أذكرها الآن تلتفت بشعرها الأسود الذي يؤطر وجهها
الناصع البياض وتنظر إليّ من تحت رموشها الطويلة ثم ترفع عينيها وتنظر إلى
الصورة. . .أذكر البلل على الرموش، لا أنسى تلك الصورة. لم أكن أعرف عندئذ
ـ وكيف أعرف؟ ـ أنها مثل أخواتي جميعا لا تنظر إلى وجهي إلا وتشعر بقلبها
يتقطع، ينفصل إلى قطعتين. . .إلى هذه اللحظة لا أنسى ملامح وجهها وكيف
تتبدل الملامح، الحب والكره والحيرة والخوف والغضب، ملامح لا أفهم كيف. . .

Confessions

My father used to kidnap people and kill them. My brother says he saw my father transform, during the war, from someone he knew to someone he didn't know. That's my big brother—I never knew my little brother. I know his picture, I know his face, he looks more like me than my big brother—that is, in photos he used to look more like me—and I call him my little brother, as all of us used to call him—in our heads, even if we didn't actually mention him in our conversations, his pictures still filled the house—what was I saying? I call him my little brother even though he isn't my little brother, and I call him "little" because he stayed that way, because he never grew up, because they killed him when he was a boy.

How many times did I see my sisters sitting silently in the living room (the safe room, our refuge in times of shelling) as if they were at a funeral, side by side on the long sofa with the green velvet cover, gazing at the enlarged picture of him on the wall, a black ribbon hanging over the corner of it. How many times did I see my big sister turn, in tears, and watch me enter carrying a sandwich—I ate sandwiches all the time: the shelling died down at sunset, and my mother would rush into the kitchen, warning me not to follow her, but I always did. I ate those mortadella and pickle sandwiches as fast as she could make them. I can recall my sister now as if all these years had not passed—they passed and they didn't—I remember her turning to look at me from beneath her long lashes, her black hair framing her white face, and I remember how she'd raise her eyes and look at the picture.... I can recall the moisture on her lashes, I haven't forgotten that. I didn't know at the time—how could I?—that my sisters weren't able to look at my face without feeling their hearts break, split in two.... To this moment I haven't forgotten my sister's face, how it transformed, the love and hate, the confusion and fear and anger. I didn't understand how her expressions could suddenly appear like that, only to melt away and be replaced by others. How could her face be so transformed in the blink of an eye? Clouds don't race that quickly across the sky.... What was she feeling when she looked at me and then at the picture? When we passed each other in the corridor, between the living room and the kitchen, my big brother often pushed me in the chest to move me out of his way, and I would turn toward him and see the strange expression on his face as he looked back at me: as if the sight of my face was repulsive to him. He'd bare his teeth like a wolf, I didn't know why.... So much time has passed and yet, even now, I still don't know how to tell my story. All of this is hard. All these years have gone by, and I'm still at a loss, still unable to speak, as if the words themselves were clogging my throat: I can feel them rising from my belly, from my heart. And as I finally speak, it feels like the mud is leaving. But it's not mud.

This memory is one of my oldest from the house in Achrafieh—it might be from the very last days of the Two-Year War, but I'm not sure of the exact date. But I know it's from that period—that much I know—from the last part of the Two-Year War, not from '75, yes, from '76, I'm sure of that, and not the beginning of '76, because at the beginning of '76 I was bedridden, feverish, caught between life and death—I didn't open my mouth back then, didn't speak a word. I was saved, a new life was written for me. What I remember from that time—the time of my illness—is dark and strange and fluid. I'll talk about it later: all of my memories from that first period are jumbled, and I don't trust them, I don't know if they're real or imagined, if they've become intertwined with dreams, if they're stories I later heard from my sisters and my big brother and my mother (my father didn't speak much). My oldest memory—the oldest one that I know belongs to me, a real memory and not someone else's invention, not my own invention either—is from the Achrafieh house: my father burning clothes and notebooks in our backyard. I can still see the fire and the wood, the stove made of large stones. I remember the fire was outside the stove, on the ground, where my mother used to set her large washing pot (the electricity went out a lot back then, and my mother and sisters would do the laundry by hand under the peach tree), and I remember my father, his darkened face—he didn't look like my father—and how his face clouded over while he pulled things—I didn't know what they were—out of a deep sackcloth and threw them onto the fire, as the tongues of flame leaped to lick his eyelids and the hair on his head. He was inching around the fire, slowly, and I stayed inside by the kitchen table, not moving a muscle, holding my breath while gazing through the open door. Even now I remember my fear. I didn't know what was happening.

But I have another memory from that period as well, a memory I love and always enjoy calling to mind: all of us were in the family room and the shelling had stopped days earlier, maybe weeks earlier, I can't be more specific, but the feeling of safety was almost complete, as if there were no threats of the cease-fire being broken at any moment, even though no one trusted the "cease-fires"... No, it actually felt like peacetime, but the war wasn't over—the Two-Year War hadn't ended yet. We were sitting there as if the war weren't happening, as if the war had never even taken place. All of us were in the family room, gathered around the wooden fold-up table as my mother poured hot *kishk* porridge into bowls. My father cut the bread and passed it around—I remember his big hands and the hair on his fingers, and my brother taking the sliced loaf from him, uncovering it, and placing a piece between him and my little sister—she always sat next to him, on his right. One of my sisters laughed as she watched. My little sister split the piece of bread in two because she didn't eat much. We were scared she was becoming anemic: she never ate anything—she liked drinking milk but didn't like eating—all this is part of the same memory: when I recall us sitting together on that distant morning, eating warm *kishk* and watching the steam rise from our bowls, which were quickly becoming empty, I remember count-less details about my sisters, brother, and parents. I remember, for example, the knife in my big sister's hand as she peeled onions, and how she cut each onion into four pieces to pass around. I remember the basket filled with onions, and how the peels were piling up. Years later, I started having unsettling dreams: I saw that very same scene, but with different faces. I saw a big stove in the middle of the room, and slices of white onion on top of the stove, slices that were turning black over the flame. I saw a loaf of bread being toasted beside the pieces of onion. The entire scene was changing before my eyes: it wasn't the Achrafieh house anymore, it was a different house. And I saw faces, at once strange and familiar. Who were they? What did the memory mean? All of this—back in that earliest period of my memories—used to torture me. Torture me? That word doesn't mean what I want it to mean. I was confused and didn't know why. I didn't know why the confusion wouldn't dissipate, why I took such an inter-est in those incomprehensible dreams.

My father didn't take part in many battles, but he kidnapped and killed I don't know how many people—sometimes a hundred or even two or three hundred people would disappear in a single day. Right here, in Beirut. "Black Saturday" was one of those days. But there were many others. I told you I spent part of the Two-Year War sick, hovering between life and death. And I told you my first memories are confused, all jumbled together. A long time passed, after the fever and the loss of all that blood, and for a long time I could only move slowly, sluggishly—my body lacked strength. I used to hold onto the table, the sofa, or the edge of the bed as I moved among the rooms of the house, not knowing where I was.

How accurate are my memories? Remembering is difficult, you can't imagine how difficult this is for me. I remember myself and I don't. It's like I'm remembering a life someone else has lived. Strange, this feeling. And at the same time not strange at all. Listen: in the first days of winter, when the cold sets in and the rains begin to fall, I always feel a pain in my chest. Every year, every single year. Often the pain in my chest is so sharp that I have to gasp for air. What do these small things reveal?

When I started college in West Beirut—after the end of the war in 1990—I thought I was entering dangerous territory. I was careful about what I said, and I noticed that I, like my father, didn't like to talk much. I didn't realize this until after I started college. I began thinking about my father a lot back then, and tried to understand him—but how can you understand someone who never stops building walls around himself? I have pictures and countless memories of my father. Sometimes these memories suffocate me. But it's Ilya's memories of him that suffocate me even more—and also my sisters' memories of him, and especially memories from early on in the war, especially those memories.

He used to disappear from the house for days and nights on end. There wasn't a single person in the entire Sioufi district who didn't know what he was up to—half the makeshift roadblocks at the crossings were of his doing. He had certain companions who never left his side, even for a moment. His reputation kept growing, until they came to know his name over there, on the other side of the demarcation line—that's what Ilya said. Was he exaggerating? If he wasn't exaggerating, if all of that was true, if... Listen: all of this is exhausting, I'll keep it as short as I can.

He kidnapped families and killed them. He kidnapped them on al-Sham Road, he kidnapped them at al-Burj Square, he kidnapped them behind the Lazariyyah Complex, and at the museum, and at Bechara al-Khoury. He kidnapped them at Sodeco Square, at the al-Sayyad circle, by the Monteverde district, he kidnapped them on the bridge in Jisr al-Basha.... He went all over the place, everywhere, kidnapping and killing, kidnapping and killing. Years later, Ilya stopped me behind the Collège des Frères in Gemmayze and showed me some bullet holes in one of the walls. "We used to gun them down right here," he said.

How many years have passed since the Two-Year War? Thirty-two? Thirty-three? As I speak now, I feel as if I'm more than one person: there's someone inside me who wants to talk and talk and talk, and there's someone else inside me who wants me to shut up, to shut up forever, to never open my mouth again.

My father used to kidnap people and kill them. In one of the narrow streets by al-Burj Square, in one of those alleys not far from the square, he stopped a white car and asked the passengers for their papers. Two men were up front, and a woman was in the back with some children. The driver was shaking—he was terrified. How had he come here? Had he entered the alley by mistake? Lost his way? Had the car brought him here of its own accord? He was terrified. And so was the passenger in the front seat. Was the woman in the back his wife? And the children... three or four children, who were they?

My father wasn't alone. He was the leader of the group. Something happened—maybe nothing happened, maybe that's how it always went down—and they opened fire on the car. The car was stopped: the road had been blocked off with barrels and with my father's car. Where could that family go? They opened fired on the car. It was raining. A light drizzle had been falling all that day, and my father and the men with him were wearing raincoats. Maybe the driver had lost his way because of the rain, because the car had a broken wiper, because he was afraid of deserted spaces. There were stores and offices in the square, and restaurants and parking lots, buildings and theaters. But this place, this alley near the square, was deserted. This was by the demarcation line. The frightened man had lost his way, the car came to a roadblock, and men in raincoats emerged from the shadows and opened fire on the people in the car.

The woman in the back held onto the children as the broken glass rained down on her. She held onto the children while the bullets spilled blood from her body. One of the armed men opened the door to the backseat to fire from close range. A little boy jumped out. He was four or five years old, blond, and fair-skinned. He was crying convulsively (warm blood was streaming from his body), he looked like he'd just woken up: that look was on his face, the look of a boy who'd been woken unwillingly from sleep.

He was wearing a white wool sweater. Blood seeped from its collar, and the stain kept on growing until it covered his whole chest. My father saw him and drew nearer to look at him. He motioned his friend away (the machine gun was still warm) and picked up the boy, who had fallen over. He wrapped the boy in a blanket and took him away.

The doctor said the boy would die from the loss of blood. But still they gave him bag after bag of blood. And they removed the bullets and shards of glass from his body. The doctor said the boy would die, and asked my father where he'd found him—the doctor knew my father—we found him on the street, my father said.

The doctor said he'd die. But the boy didn't die. His wounds became infected; his fever rose. They thought there was no hope for him. But he didn't die. When he was finally better, when he opened his eyes to find himself lying on a bed in a house and not in a hospital, he didn't open his mouth. He opened his eyes and looked at the faces that were looking at him. He heard words coming from a distance, but didn't understand what he was seeing and hearing. Did they ask him what his name was then? Maybe no one asked him. He was four or five years old, and had come back from death. He was cured, and my father named him Maroun.

—*He named him after you?*

No. I'm Maroun. I'm the boy they kidnapped.

Charles-Ferdinand Ramuz, born in Lausanne in 1878, is one of Switzerland's pro-lific modernists. Though French was his mother tongue, Ramuz felt estranged from the language. His body of work is a testament to this estrangement and an attempt to allow the particular rhythms of his country to enter Francophone literature.

Jean-Luc persécuté

Il y avait un air épais, bleu autour de la lampe qui pendait au plafond; où ils étaient sept ou huit hommes, serrés à une table, Jean-Luc au milieu d'eux. Il avait fait venir un premier litre, qui était bu; il en fit venir un deuxième, qui fut bientôt vide, lui aussi; alors il cria: «Encore un!» qu'on apporta. Et il le souleva, ayant sorti sa bourse qu'il soupesait de l'autre main; il reprit: «C'est encore elle la plus lourde.»

—C'est que je suis riche! continua-t-il.

Et tout à coup vida son argent sur la table. Les écus se mirent à rouler que les autres les retenaient au passage, les posant à plat devant eux; ils les comptaient, disant: «D'où est-ce que tu as tout ça?» et regardaient Jean-Luc avec crainte et respect.

—Secret! répondait Jean-Luc.

Il parlait haut, d'une voix assurée; il fouilla dans sa poche, il en tira deux billets de banque.

—Et ça? qu'il dit en riant.

Et il cria:

—Encore un litre!

Mais soudain, ils se mirent tous à rire, le cordonnier étant entré. Il s'appelait Nanche, c'était un tout petit homme chauve, noir de figure et noir des mains, avec un tablier vert; deux jours par semaine, à peu ...

The Persecution of Jean-Luc

The air was thick, blue around the lamp that hung from the ceiling; they were about seven or eight men, cramped around a table, Jean-Luc in the middle. He had ordered a first liter, which was now finished; he ordered a second, which was soon emptied too; then he cried: "Another one!" which they brought. And he lifted it up while he took out his purse, which he held in the other hand; he went on: "This is still heavier."

—It's because I'm rich! he continued.

And suddenly emptied his money on the table. The crowns began to roll, the others caught them as they went by, laying them down flat before them; they counted them, saying: "Where'd you get all this money from?" and looked at Jean-Luc with fear and respect.

—That's a secret! answered Jean-Luc.

He spoke loudly, in a confident voice; he rummaged through his pocket, he took out two bank bills.

—What about these? he said, laughing.

And he cried:

—Another liter!

But suddenly, they all started to laugh, the cobbler having entered. His name was Nanche, he was a very small man, bald, with a black face and black hands, and a green apron; he would only work about two days a week; the rest of the time, he tended to his thirst, as he said, and added: "It's the leather that dries me up."

He had gone to sit alone in a corner, they called to him:

—Hey! Nanche, you sulking?

He did not move, still sober. But because Jean-Luc had started to make his crowns resound again, now Nanche turned his head from time to time, taking a sideways look at the money that shone—and shrugged his shoulders.

Upon which, it was Jean-Luc's turn to call him:

—Come on, Nanche! We miss you.

Nanche did not respond anything at first; then, when he finished his bottle of eau-de-vie, he suddenly stood up and came over. His eyes shone beneath his big drooping eyebrows, while he dried his hands on his apron. He said:

—Hello, gang!

—Hurray for us! cried Jean-Luc.

He made him take a seat near him and at once made him drink.

—Here's to you, he started again; when one is happy one drinks well, when one drinks well one is happy.

The noise went on increasing, as well as the smoke; they could barely see one another in the small room, with its great beams that seemed to weigh down on their heads, they spoke of anything, in any which way—the men leaning on their elbows all along the table, their heads down, looking out of the corners of their eyes, and they ran their hands over their moustaches; within the group, Nanche, smaller than everyone else, and Jean-Luc, pale, who laughed.

And, having made him drink once more, he patted Nanche on the back:

—Now you're going to sing us something.

Which is what everyone was waiting for, because that was how it went: when he was drunk, they did with him what they liked, they went so far as to hang him by the thumbs, as once happened, smudging his face, blackening it with tar—all this just to anger him, because that was when the fun began.

—You're going to sing us something! said Jean-Luc.

Nanche stood up on the bench, he coughed two or three times, like he always did. He began:

You've got your blonde, I've got my brunette,
I wouldn't want it any other way . . .

It was always the same song, one they all knew well; and Jean-Luc took up the refrain, which all the others burst into after him:

I prefer my brunette, ô gué,
I prefer my bru-u-nette

—Is that right? said Jean-Luc, looking up.

He added:

—Maybe so.

And, during the following refrain, he sang even louder. At that same moment, someone pulled the bench; Nanche fell flat on his back. They laughed up a storm. He had stood up quickly and cried, clenching his fists:

—Don't touch me! Don't touch me!

But already Jean-Luc had sat him back down:

—You're wasting your time, you're better off drinking.

Thus Nanche drank some more, and Jean-Luc laughed, saying:

—It's because we're joyous and happy, I tell you, and have jolly hearts, and are full of trust.

To which the others responded:

—Of course!

But, once again, in response to a sign someone made, Nanche was surrounded, taken, squeezed, snatched, hoisted to the ceiling, banged up there two or three times against the beams, then abruptly released; and found himself sprawled out on the floor, where he remained a moment, stunned. Then, having come back to his senses, he threw himself at those who were there, without knowing who they were, head down. At first no one could see a thing anymore, for there was great disorder; finally, the door having been opened, Nanche reappeared, he was shoved outside—and, slipping on the stairs, he rolled through the mud; upon which, the door was shut again. Everyone cried and coughed with laughter.

And Nanche shouted from outside:

—Thieves! Assassins!

While Jean-Luc started up again:

—It's because we've got light jolly hearts.

But soon everything hushed; the square was now empty.

—You'll see, someone said, he'll come back with his leather knife.

Upon which, they all went back to the window again. Indeed, Nanche returned, head bare, walking with difficulty, his clothes full of mud; and he went to sit at the tilden tree's bench, sharpening his blade with a stone; he spoke the whole time, but no one could understand what he was saying. And tall Laurent, opening the window, shouted:

—Hey! Nanche, come here and talk it over with us!

He came over, he was shaking with fury, he was lifting his iron; suddenly his head went through the open window, with one arm thrown forward, and the lamplight flashed on the leather knife; then the door, which was locked, was shaken, and the wood sounded beneath his kicks; following which, there was a silence, they heard something like sobbing.

—There you go, said tall Laurent, now he's crying.

And so, at the table, where they had all gone to sit back down, great laughs started up again. Except that Jean-Luc no longer laughed; he had pushed his glass back and placed both elbows on the table, his head in his hands. They said to him:

—Hey! Jean-Luc! What's up? You're not drinking anymore.

He said no, then, throwing down the coin he had taken out, he asked: "What does it matter?" paid, took his change, and headed for the door. They cried to him:

—Be careful!

But he did not listen.

Nanche was sitting on the front steps. Jean-Luc approached him, nudged him with his elbow, and said:

—I was wrong, you see, because we're brothers.

Then he held out his hand to him. The cobbler looked up, and in the gleam of the window, they stared into each other's faces. And Nanche said:

—Come with me.

Jean-Luc followed him. It rained from a low sky that weighed down on roofs; the sky barely prevailed, due to a moon crescent lost behind the clouds, a lack of clarity in the air, and within it the houses were square and black. They walked together, linking arms. And when they were at Nanche's house, at the other end of the square, he went on:

—You have to come in.

And so Jean-Luc did, and he repeated:

—We're brothers.

—Is that true? said Nanche, who was now sitting down. They've taken my honor.

Jean-Luc responded:

—Mine too, they've taken my honor too.

Nanche had his bed in what looked like a kitchen, a straw mattress laid out on the floor; one of the table's legs was missing, this leg had been replaced by an upright crate; on the hearth, near the marmite of polenta, there was a pot of pea fondue; spiderwebs hung all about.

They became friends, Nanche having said:

—You're right.

They sat side by side before the hearth. They had blown on the ash, where there remained a few embers that came back to life, and the bundle of sticks blazed. Jean-Luc said:

—Are you here for me? Maybe so, because, you see, we were six children, and three are dead, and, of the other three, two are far, and my father too is dead and I chased off my wife, and as for the child, they say he isn't mine.

Nanche repeated:

—So then, is it true that we're brothers?

He shook his head:

—It's like Our Lord, they shared his robe amongst themselves, they beat him, whipped him, they spit in his face, they put him on a cross.

And in the light of the bright flame, which trembled on the walls:

—Well, they beat me, knocked me out, and they say amongst themselves: "He's crying." I answer them: "What are eyes for?"

But Jean-Luc shouted in a terrible voice:

—And they kneel before money! Look, look what I do with it!

He had taken the bills that were in his pocket, he held them out to the flame. It bit into their corners, spread rapidly; and, the paper having slipped from his fingers, fell into the cinders. Only a bit of white ash remained, which Jean-Luc crushed with his feet. Nanche had not moved an inch. He only said:

—It's really burning up!

Then they remained without speaking, still very close to one another. The stillness of night encircled the house. And Jean-Luc felt his rage die down, and, the wine haze having dispersed in his head, what he needed now was to rest and to have someone near him, and he thought: "I've got someone here," thinking of Nanche—but, having turned around, he realized that Nanche had fallen asleep. He slept, his head against Jean-Luc's shoulder. And Jean-Luc, pulling out the straw mattress, laid him out on the straw mattress.

And so, once again, he was alone. He was completely alone with himself. And once again he was no longer sure of anything. Yet, when Nanche writhed in his dreams, crying: "Leave me alone!" suddenly sitting up, waving his arms—each time Jean-Luc went to him and put him back to bed. Then, in the end, he yielded to sleep; he lay down at Nanche's side. He slept until morning.

When he came home, his back was all white and spiderwebs were caught at the brim of his hat. He walked along the houses, with his red eyes, and a fire in his head. He told people: "The most evil ones are not the ones you think."

—You say: I drink. Ah well! Yes, I do drink. But is there a sparkle in my glass? They've got a hard heart, you see.

When he arrived in front of his house, he heard the blacksmith calling to him:

—Hey! Jean-Luc, he said, it can't go on like this, your little one has spent all night at ours, and my wife already has four children.

For a moment, he hesitated, then he responded:

—Leave me the hell alone!

—Don't listen to everything people say! continued the blacksmith.

But Jean-Luc shook his head and, without adding anything, closed the door behind him.

That afternoon, he drank again; this time he went to sit alone in a corner with Nanche; he said: "We understand each other." Nanche had something like respect for him; they remained together all evening. And, when tall Laurent approached to start his teasing again, Jean-Luc looked him straight in the eye and said:

—Don't touch him anymore, you understand, I'm here now!

He no longer left the inn, he was never at home anymore. So that he was not there to receive his mother the day she came, a week later. Having heard the rumors regarding her son, the money thrown afar, his passion for drinking, and besides, being even more self-interested than proud, she had told herself: "I must go." She found Félicie in the kitchen with the little one; and the poor thing did not grasp who she was, nor had she the concerns of orderly women, for that requires reason: the bed was not made, clothes were scattered across the room; there was a strong stench and great filthiness; the little one had cried, the tears on his cheeks had crusted into white lines. The old woman said to Félicie: "Be off!" She chased her away. She rolled up her skirt, scrubbed and cleaned until evening.

At that moment, Jean-Luc returned. There came the loud sound of voices, which quickly ceased; then old Philomène came back down the stairs, and she went back through the entire village, having no choice, but without speaking to anyone, nor turning around.

Jean-Luc went on drinking. And another piece of his meadow sold for a little money Craux gave him (who kept an eye on him now); it was one of the best pieces, the one in Roussettes, which he cared about; but he did not seem to regret the way his property dismantled itself, piece by piece, being so disconnected from it all. To such an extent that, one day, having run into Augustin, when the latter made a detour, he cried to him:

—Take the shortest way, I have no desire to lay a hand on you.

He no longer even had any respect for religion, or so it seemed, for he no longer attended mass; the beautiful season now here, the processions had started again, making the rounds of the cemetery; he remained standing behind the wall, watching, and they heard him say: "It's all playacting!"

Yet the new spring was bright and gay, it seemed to rinse the heart, the vines had never been so beautiful, which explained the contentment—along with the crops and the wheat of a good height, and the grass early grown. Even the clouds are pleasant to watch, small and white in the sky, like daisies in grass; a tall woman passed by on the road, carrying a lamb in her arms.

People greeted one another before the crosses. The bisse men came home from work in packs, with their pickaxes and their shovels over their shoulders, they removed their hats when they walked by the cross. They had returned water to the bisse. The streams, all swollen, twirling along the thaw's yellow water, jumped over the bridges one day, then declined and went dry. The toads, on humid nights, stroll down the paths.

Jean-Luc went on drinking. Félicie watched over the little one. She would go to sit by the pond beneath a willow. The bank comes down steeply toward the water, which is immediately deep, and black in its depth; but, at the surface, it glimmers, with the blue of the sky, the white of the snow, the green of the meadows; and there are also the reflections of the little trees and of the bushes leaning over the water, such as the willow Félicie sat under.

The little Henri played near her, rolling his ball of thread; or he climbed onto her lap, and having put down her knitting, she started to sing.

But other times, too, she seemed to get lost outside of herself in things, with eyes that no longer saw anything, fixed on a point in the immensity before her, her spirit in flight afar; the house was empty over there; the little one, left alone, ran after the grasshoppers.

Born in the same year as Octavio Paz, Efraín Huerta (1914–1982) has come to be recognized as a pivotal figure in modern Mexican poetry. His influence on later Mexican poets continues to grow. Writes Octavio Paz of him: "Efraín Huerta has a central place in the poetry of the modern city."

Poemínimos

Optimismo

Si tengo
Suerte
Llegaré
En un
Poeminitaxi

Planes I

Cuando
Yo sea
Muy rico
Voy a poner
Un servicio
De
    Poeminitaxis

Poemínimos

Optimism

With some
Luck
I'll come'n
Get you
In a
Poeminitaxi
Honey

Plans I

When
I get
Very rich
I'm gonna roll out
A whole fleet
Of
    Poeminitaxis

Planes II

Todos
Los hacen
Para un
Borroso futuro

Yo los hago
Para un
Siniestro
Pero clarísimo
        Pasado

El cómico

Regularmente
Hago
Una
Vida
Bastante
Irregular

Plans II

All of you
Make them
For a
Fuzzy old future

I make mine
For a
Creepy
But spic & span
      Past

The Comic

Regularly
I make
A
Life
Irregular
Enough

Tláloc

Sucede
Que me canso
De ser dios
Sucede
Que me canso
De llover
Sobre mojado

Sucede
Que aquí
Nada sucede
Sino la lluvia
      lluvia
      lluvia
      lluvia

Tlaloc (the Rain God)

Happens
That I'm tired
Of being God
Happens
That I'm tired
Of it raining
When it's damp

Happens
That there's nothing
Here that happens
But the rain
      The rain
      The rain
      The rain

Ángel I

El
Ángel
Al
Elevadorista:
"Lléveme
Al
Último
Piso.
Después
Sigo
Solo."

Ángel II

Y
Si
Me
Caigo
    Qué
Del
Cielo
No
Paso

Angel I

The
Angel
To the
Elevator
Operator:
"Take
Me
To the
Top
Floor.
Then
I'll go on
Solo."

Angel II

And
If
I
Fall down
      What
Part of
Sky
Won't I
Pass

Revelación

Alguien
Revelaba:
"Las tardes
En que
Me siento
Incapaz
De ser
Inteligente
Finjo
Que me
Aburro."

Distancia

Del
Dicho
Al
Lecho
Hay
Mucho
Trecho

Revelation

Someone
Reveals:
"Those evenings
When
I feel
Incapable
Of being
Smart
I just pretend
I'm being
Bored."

Distances

From the
Said
To the
Bed
There's
Plenty of
Spread

Tótem

Siempre
Amé
Con la
Furia
Silenciosa
De un
Cocodrilo
Aletargado

Totem

I always
Loved
With the
Silent
Fury
Of a
Somnolent
Crocodile

I. Grekova, pseudonym of Elena Sergeevna Venttsel' (1907–2002), was a mathematician. Her name incorporates the mathematic variable y (igrek in Russian). Along with textbooks and professional studies, she wrote three novels, six novellas, and numerous stories reflecting life in the Soviet Union, especially for women.

Свежо предание

Первым впечатлением, которое он запомнил, был радужный солнечный зайчик на стене. Обои были светлые, в крупных косых клетках, и в самую середину одной из клеток упал зайчик и лежал там, не шевелясь, притихший и полосатый, сияющий каждым цветом.

Маленький мальчик еще толком не знал названий цветов—ему было всего три года. Он засмеялся и стал ловить зайчик рукой. Зайчик не давался: он только лег сверху на желтоватую худенькую руку и чуть-чуть изменил цвета. Мальчик был счастлив.

Он сидел на постели у мамы, на подушке, между мамой и зайчиком. Он давно не видел маму: она куда-то исчезла, а потом вернулась, и вот сейчас, сидя на подушке, он был ужасно счастлив, весь дрожал от счастья и от страха, что мама снова уйдет. Мама лежала желтая и бледная, та и не та, не совсем знакомая, остриженная, с короткой щетинкой на черной круглой голове. Малыш трогал щетинку пальцем, узнавал маму и боялся себе поверить и на всю жизнь запомнил радужный зайчик на светлых обоях и ощущение счастья, смешанное со страхом, что оно уйдет....

The Tale Is Fresh

The first impression that lodged in his memory was a rainbow-edged spot of light on the wall. The wallpaper was pale, with large slanting checks, and the light spot fell in the very middle of one of the checks and lay there without stirring, quiet and striped, shining with every color.

The little boy still didn't know the names of the colors well—he was only three years old. He laughed and started trying to catch the light spot with his hand. The light spot wouldn't let him catch it: it just lay on top of his thin yellowish arm and changed colors ever so slightly. The boy was happy.

He was sitting on mama's bed, on a pillow, between mama and the spot of light. He hadn't seen mama for a long time: she had disappeared somewhere, and then came back, and right now, sitting on the pillow, he was terribly happy, all trembling from happiness and from fear that mama might go away again. She was lying there, sallow and pale, herself and not herself, not entirely familiar, with her hair cut, short bristles on her round black head. The little boy touched the bristles with his finger, recognized that it was his mother, and was afraid to believe it. And he remembered for his whole life the rainbow spot of light on the pale wallpaper and the feeling of happiness, mixed with fear that it would go away.

Afterward, much later, he found out that it had happened in the year 1920, that mama had been sick with typhus and had almost died, and the rainbow spot of light came from the crystal ashtray on the table. It was a big ashtray made of clear, heavy crystal with smooth gleaming facets. When the boy got bigger, he learned to move the ashtray himself on sunny days and to send the spot of light along the wall. And so a rainbow spot of light danced over his childhood, his life, but then it started to appear more and more rarely, until finally it went out altogether.

The boy's name was Konstantin Levin.

His parents—Izaak Levin and Vera Bergman—had met in 1912 at a student party. He was studying engineering, she was in the Bestuzhev courses for women. Both of them were young, even very young. Both were revolutionaries. Both had gone into the revolution because it was impossible to live in any other way.

Vera was merry, black-haired, with round trustful eyes and finely waving hair, such a fine wave that it didn't even seem fluffy. When she opened her mouth to laugh, her pale blue teeth stood in an even row like peas in a pod. She spoke with a very sweet guttural burr, and every "r" leaped and jingled in her throat like a little round bell. Vera often laughed, she liked to be with people, she was hard to embitter and easy to console, and she was firm as a rock in misfortune. A laughing flint pebble. When you strike it, it gives off laughter and sparks.

Many people thought she was frivolous. And it was hard to guess, no one would have guessed, that this light, laughing, merry Vera carried an unchanging, horrible image with her, hiding it deep inside. It was the image of two dead people—her grandfather and Tsilya.

Her grandfather and her little sister Tsilya had been killed in a pogrom in 1905, when Very was twelve. Her grandfather was lying on his back, head turned to one side, his gray beard sticking out to the side. He was motionless, but it seemed as if he was running, desperately hurrying, and his beard had been blown to one side by the wind. And across her grandfather's wide chest lay little Tsilya, with a blue face, her black curls in little ringlets. Grandfather was holding her, as if to protect her and carry her away with him—in his old man's arm, white and very skinny with blue veins.

This picture always lay before her. All Vera had to do was fall silent, get pensive, simply stop laughing, and something inside her would slip off—like a pendulum swinging toward its point of balance—and once again grandfather and Tsilya would be lying there, on the ground splattered with red. The moment she was off her guard they were there again. Grandfather and Tsilya.

At first it made her want to shout, bite her hands, but gradually Vera almost got used to them. And the picture itself changed with the years, grew more peaceful, and now in her memory grandfather lay more motionless, and his beard wasn't blown quite as much to the side by the wind. But the image was always inside her, and it was because of them that Vera went into the revolution: grandfather and Tsilya. It was impossible for things to be that way. Something had to be done so that it wouldn't be that way.

Vera saw Izya Levin for the first time at the door of the little apartment where a get-together had been scheduled. She rang the bell, and he opened the door. She had been running up the stairs, afraid she was being tailed; she was panting, and coming from the frost outside into the warm. She had long eyelashes and batted them to shake off the snowflakes.

On the threshold stood a tall, swarthy young man, slender as a whip, with enormous, light eyes that were merry to the point of insolence. These eyes were what stuck most in her memory, and also his tousled brown hair, damp in front, sticking to his forehead. He was wearing a white, gleaming Tolstoyan shirt and a twisted silk belt with ornamental tufts. A student's jacket hung by some kind of miracle on one shoulder. In his hand, a guitar.

"I'm Vera Bergman," she said. The little bell rolled and jingled twice in her throat.

The student looked at her, his eyes laughing with furious joy, but he didn't say his name. Instead of greeting her, he moved the guitar into his other hand, brought his index finger up to his lips, then very quickly and without any constraint put it on one of Vera's cheeks, then the other, and said twice, "Tss! Tss!" as if he had burned himself.

"Like testing an iron?" asked Vera.

"Exactly. Clever girl. You understand everything."

"Well then . . . " said Vera, abashed, and stole a look in the mirror. And indeed, her cheeks were red as fire from the cold, with a light fuzz, and probably just adorable.

But he was a strange one, all the same . . .

Meanwhile the strange student quickly, gracefully, and just as unconstrainedly helped her take off her velvet jacket, her fur hat, took her little muff, and he hung and put all that down, turning this way and that way, flexible, slender, flapping the black wing of his hanging jacket, which had also figured out how to dance, hanging on his shoulder in some mysterious way. All this was a bit over the top. There was too much movement for the simple task he was doing. It seemed as if any moment his waist might snap.

He flung the door wide open and bowed, letting her go through ahead.

The room—not quite a dining room, not quite a living room—was thick with smoke; the samovar was singing, cups were clattering. The hostess—a thin, freckled young woman with a horsy face and a pince-nez that hung on some kind of reins—barely noticed Vera, quickly gave her hand a shake, said, "Amuse yourself independently. We don't stand on ceremony. Some tea?" and, without waiting for an answer, went back to the debaters.

The argument was humming like a hive of bumblebees. Tobacco smoke marched over the tea table with the dirty plates, soggy cigarette butts, bloodless lemon slices in unfinished glasses of tea. What was the debate about? She could hear "The State Duma...Markov the Second...the Beilis case...medical expertise...international scandal...the Beilis case..."

Suddenly one person who stood out from the group of debaters—a hefty man with a black beard—lifted a hand as broad as a frying pan, and announced in a powerful bass that drowned out the argument, "That's not the main thing now. The important thing now is theory. There's no revolution, no struggle without theory."

But Vera didn't understand anything about theory. It seemed to her, most likely out of naivety, that you didn't need any theory. Do you really need a theory to love and to hate? She had joined the revolution because she couldn't do anything else. And also because they were lying there forever: her dead grandfather and dead Tsilya. But she never spoke about that to anyone. She couldn't let anyone in to the place where they lay.

Sitting on the couch and barely listening to the debate, she looked around, her lively eyes flashing. No, it seemed he wasn't here—the comrade she had agreed to meet. To whom she was supposed to say prearranged words (if only she didn't forget!). Who was supposed to give her letters from the Center. She wasn't acquainted with any of the faces around her. The only one who seemed familiar—frighteningly familiar—was the student who had opened the door for her and burned himself on her cheeks. He kept appearing here and there around the room—quick, mobile, eyes burning, flapping the wing of his jacket, bending first to one person, then to another, and suddenly he stopped in front of her, put his foot on a chair, seized the guitar firmly and precisely, tapped his knuckles on the soundboard, plucked the strings—once, twice... And at once the debating voices were drowned out. The strings began to ache with a penetrating tenderness...

"Well then!" he cried under his breath and broke into a rapid, stifled patter, rushing forward:

In the field a little birch tree stood...
In the field the curly birch tree stood...

he informed her confidentially, in a half whisper, as if it were who knows what kind of news (only for you, only for you!). And the guitar kept fluttering in his hands, twisting, jumping.

I'll break the white birch tree...

he informed her in the same way, as a secret, looking fiercely into Vera's eyes. "He'll break it," she started to believe, "oh, he'll break it!"

"There we go," he said, once he finished the song and sat down beside her. "Let's drink some tea."

Everything was blue-gray with smoke, and there were cigarette butts lying everywhere: in the saucers, on the windowsills, in the glasses with the lemon slices. The debates were soggy and yellow too, like the cigarette butts, and Vera didn't understand any of it, but the merry student was beside her: he would jump up, sit back down, pick up the guitar, and put it away—restless as fire in the wind. But strangely, his restlessness made her feel calm. That other comrade still hadn't come in. That should have worried Vera but it didn't, everything was fine, and she wasn't even afraid when around midnight the bell rang—long, demanding—and someone said, "The police!" There was a bit of a commotion, someone gasped, someone broke a glass, the hostess suggested that they should all keep their presence of mind, while the hefty blackbeard went to open the door. Vera herself had no idea how she wound up in the corridor, and then in the kitchen, with that same student.

"Put your things on quickly," he ordered in a whisper, holding her jacket and hat for her. "I couldn't find your muff. Can you manage without it?"

"No doubt."

"Now I'll get you out of here. You aren't afraid?"

"No."

He sharply pulled the window frame inward, it flew open wide with a dry paper snap. Outside breathed the dark, damp air of early winter. The snow had already stopped, and after the smoky room, the unexpected freshness of the night air went into their lungs like a delicate happiness.

The student jumped up on the windowsill like a cat and pulled Vera up behind him. Outside the window was a sloping roof, powdered with snow that was very white in the darkness. It rang under their feet like a bucket.

They ran across the roof, went down the fire stairs, climbed onto another roof, then a third . . . Then Vera had no more idea where they were and what roofs and ladders they were taking. Up and down . . . The student led her by the hand, sometimes carefully lifted her or helped her down. He went lightly and confidently in the darkness, with a catlike, sensitive step. Vera would not have been surprised if he had dropped from the roof, flipped over like a cat and landed right on his feet. She wasn't afraid—on the contrary, she felt cheerful and curious: how would all this end?

In the end they had to jump off a low shed roof right into the soft, fluffy snow, which settled under their feet. The courtyard was deep, dark, without a light in the windows. He jumped first and caught Vera right in his arms—thin, strong, with hard muscular knobs at the shoulders. They stood that way, locked in a hug, knee-deep in snow, catching their breath and listening.

"I guess that's it," he said. "I don't hear anyone coming after us. Well, how are you?"

"Great."

"Great," he teased, trying to roll the little bell of the "r." And suddenly, without letting go or holding her more tightly, he kissed her cold lips that smelled of thaw and snow.

"Is it all right that I did that so soon?" he asked and opened his arms.

Vera didn't answer; for some reason she started laughing. She just stood there and laughed, loudly, carefree, slapping her palms against her knees. Her knees were low, right against the snow. Actually, he was standing knee-deep in the snow and also, probably, looked like a shorty. Was she laughing at him?

"What is it?" he asked, fairly offended. "If you didn't like it, slap me and we're done."

"No, it's all right. It just seemed very funny. I don't even know what your name is."

"I'm Izya. Izaak Ruvimovich. Izaak Ruvimovich Levin. Got it?"

"Got it. Ruvimovich," she said, and suddenly put her head on his shoulder. He gave her a slight hug.

"And I don't know your patronymic."

"Oh, it's very simple. Ilyinishna."

"Ilyinishna," he said pompously, carefully, and kissed her again. "From some fairytale: Ilyinishna. We have to go, Ilyinishna. Only where?"

"Does it matter? Somewhere."

"They're watching my apartment. Otherwise I'd invite you."

"Funny. They're watching mine too."

"Then you know where let's go? To the train station."

They sat at the station until morning. And in the morning, when they said good-bye, not knowing whether they'd see each other again, they already knew everything about each other. And the main thing was, there was no need to say anything—everything was clear without it. Izya was the first one she let in there—to grandfather and Tsilya. She didn't say it in words—he already knew everything about her.

"My Nonsensishna," he said, kissing her good-bye.

Two weeks later they got married, and two weeks after that Izaak Levin was arrested. They managed to meet again only in 1916, when Izya was released from prison and almost immediately sent to the front. He spent only two weeks in Petrograd. They only lived together for two weeks, twice, before the revolution. It was all right—they were young. Their happiness lay ahead of them. It was waiting for the revolution—and the revolution came.

The boy was three years old in 1920, but he was born in 1917, in Petrograd, at the very same time as the February revolution.

Vera Levina was walking down the street on a windy winter evening, gasping at the wind, and with excitement. Here, finally, it was beginning, it had started! Here it was—the Revolution! The very same one they had fought for, died for, spent time in prisons, escaped from exile and hard labor. Was it really? It was! All the horrors were in the past: the police, the gendarmes, and those terrifying drunk ones, with their hiccups and "God Save the Tsar," who had killed grandfather and Tsilya. Nothing like that would ever happen again! The revolution had always been in the future, but now it was here, here it was, you could touch it with your hand. Revolution on the streets of Petrograd! The sky shook and burned with an amber smoky glow, and here and there shots cracked merrily, harmless and not at all frightening. Vera tried to see, as she used to, grandfather and Tsilya, but the image she always saw had gone fuzzy, slipped to one side. And what she did manage to see wasn't the same—not alive, not terrifying. It was as if grandfather had stopped running and was lying peacefully on the ground, stretching out his long legs, while Tsilya didn't want to appear at all—she flickered for a minute and disappeared. "Have they really let me go?" Vera thought. That was just as unlikely as the revolution.

Logs were piled up on the corner, under a torn-off sign that flapped loudly in the wind: a barricade. An aged, solidly bearded soldier in a fur hat, grunting, was piling the logs higher. Vera stopped beside him.

"Soldier, say, soldier," she said.

"What is it?" the soldier answered reluctantly.

"How is it?" she asked.

She herself didn't know "how is it." Maybe she wanted the soldier to confirm her joy, her pride. To praise her for the revolution, or something.

"You should be away from here, miss," the soldier said gloomily.

Then something incomprehensible happened. She heard a kind of cold, fine chirp, not outside—no, but inside her, in herself. Vera thought the chirp was funny, but something in her chest stopped her from laughing. She waved her mitten at the soldier and softly, her boots slipping, started to fall to one side against the beams. Suddenly she saw her grandfather: alive, laughing, with a handsome beard. He was sitting on the chair under the clock, and little Tsilya sat on his lap, playing with his watch chain.

The soldier bent over. He saw her pale face, blue-tinged, the rounded lids on her partly closed eyes, and out of the corner of her mouth—a wavering black string: blood.

"Oh Lord, they've wounded her. Mother of God," he said, catching Vera under her arms. The little miss turned out to be unexpectedly heavy. So that's what it was . . .

"Ah, you little birdie," the soldier said bitterly and protectively.

He picked Vera up in his arms and took her off to an army field hospital. That night they operated on her, and toward morning Konstantin Levin was born.

"It's you, it's you," Izaak Levin repeated pointlessly, kneeling beside Vera's cot, kissing the rough woolen blanket. He was thin and scary, with white lips, in a short fur coat with a Mauser at his belt. He'd come home from the front for one day, and the next day he had to go back. Perhaps he had even deserted—Vera didn't quite understand. She was lying with her weak arms spread on top of the blanket, but for some reason he wasn't kissing her hands but the blanket, and he kept repeating: "It's you." Suddenly he remembered the baby boy. The boy was superfluous, unreal, had no significance. Only she existed, Vera—alive!

"How's the boy," he asked. In essence, he wasn't concerned with the boy. He asked in essence just out of politeness.

A little smile fluttered on Vera's pale lips.

"He's very nice, very nice," she answered in a whisper. "I have no milk. What should we call him?"

"Doesn't matter," said Izaak. "It's you."

And Vera named the boy Konstantin.

And did she ever get it for that from Izya, when they finally saw each other! The boy was already six months old when his father found out for the first time what his name was.

"What lack of forethought!" shouted Izaak. "Konstantin Levin! Why not just call him Evgenii Onegin? Or Childe Harold? You've disgraced him for his whole life. Everyone's going to ask him: has it been a long time since you made your appearance in the novel *Anna Karenina*?"

"I just forgot," Vera said, laughing.

"Forgot what?"

"That there's an Anna Karenina. That there's a Konstantin Levin."

"Konstantin, and on top of that Izaakovich! A very attractive combination! Did you think at all about what they'd call him when he grew up?"

"No, I didn't think," Vera answered flippantly. "Maybe when he grows up there won't be any more patronymics. But for now everyone calls him Tang-Tin. As if he's Chinese. Isn't that nice?"

Nonsensishna!" Izaak thundered. "You really are a proper Nonsensishna! By the way, where is that paradox? I haven't even seen him yet."

"He's lying on the balcony, blue with happiness."

"Why blue?"

"Go see for yourself."

They went out on the balcony. And indeed, there was Tang-Tin in a laundry basket, blue with happiness. He was drunk, dead drunk on the fresh cool air, he was sleeping desperately, passionately, ecstatically, with fine transparent blue eyelids, with blue veins on his little white temples.

"Konstantin Izaakovich," Izya suddenly said tenderly. "An absurdity and son of an absurdity."

"That's much better," said Vera with approval. "Well, and now take me in your arms."

He took her in his arms, and they stood quietly beside the laundry basket, attentively watching as Tang-Tin labored with his inspired sleep. Without words they thought about the world he would live in, where there would be no more passports, and perhaps not even patronymics, and where no one would ask little Tang-Tin whether he was a Jew or not and why he was Izaakovich.

Minoru Yoshioka (1919–1990) was one of the most important poets of Japan's postwar period. Influenced by Modernism and Surrealism, he developed an experimental poetry that involved a creative dialogue with butoh dance and painting. His later work focused on the practice of appropriation and collage.

Minoru Yoshioka | A FABLE

寓話

肉屋の千匹の蠅　と飛び終り　包丁刃物の類は　仮設の暗がり
から　あとずさりして　一段と深い世界へ沈みゆき

慰めのない　真夏の仕事場　凍る肉の重い柱　さかさにつる
される　完全に浄められた空間　すでに人間のはげしい咀
嚼の音もとおざかり

今この店先の調理台のうえに　尾もない頭もない　一つの肉
の原型　魅せられたように　よこたわって

すべてのものの耳がゆれ立ち
すべてのものの舌が巻かれる時

苦痛の鈎からはずれた凝脂の肉の神
虚しい過去　生の真昼の空を夢みようとする

甘い太陽とみどりの草　臓腑の中で輝く　河
と星眉　角の間くぼうぼう風をとばし　疾走
する四肢の下で　みだれる夕焼の雲　小鳥の
脱糞　金の糞の中で　つねに反芻される　自
我のエクスタシイ

A Fable

The thousand flies in the butcher shop——stop flying   the various
    kinds of knives   walk backwards   out of the makeshift
    darkness   and sink into a deeper world

The workplace in midsummer   without comfort   the heavy
    columns of frozen meat   hung upside down   in the
    completely purified space   the intense sound of
    humans chewing grows distant
On the countertop at the front of the store   the prototype of a
    piece of meat   with no   head or tail   lies down   as if
    enchanted

All ears rock back and forth on their feet
The time when all tongues wind up

The god of meat with solidified oil that escaped the bitter hook
Tries to dream of a sky in the noon of life   his empty past

        Sweet sun and green grass   river   and stardust
        Sparkling in the guts   wind blowing through horns

凶悪な笑
柔媚な
その尻の穴をほそめてゆく
嫣然と眦を
放尿の海
とぎに牝の
汚れた鼻づらで冒す
混清の涎
渹沱たる
地平の端を
いと
紅の座を嚼きつけ
時一ああ果は

主人の描ものそかぬ　化石めいた深夜のホリント　すなわ
ち店先の部厚い矩形の処刑台をきしませ　裂かれた肉の衣
装のかげから　触発されたもの　突然立ち上がりよみがえり
みるみる形成されだす　裸の牡牛の像

くばりついた梁で　夜あけまでみぶるいする　肉屋の千匹の
蠅

Below the scampering four legs   scattered sunset clouds
A little bird defecates   in the golden straw, always
     ruminating
Chewing its cud   the self's ecstasy
To the edge of the horizon he ventures with dirty nose ring
An atrocious laugh and   confused slobber   at times
Snorting at the assholes of cows   fawning over the
     crimson throne
Gracefully narrowing his eyes—then
He ends up here   in this sea of abundant urination

A stage backdrop of fossilized night   not even the owner's cat
     dares take a peek
The massive rectangular scaffold at the front of the store, and
     the grinding sounds as the meat is cut and cleaved to pieces
     from the shadows of its costume   something is suddenly
     inspired to stand up, to rise from the dead
     and in no time it begins to form   the figure of a naked bull

On the beams   trembling till dawn   the butcher shop's one
     thousand flies

ジャングル

木が茂る　実は熟れる　茂るまま枯れる
沈黙の中で　或は形而上の外で　実がおちる
枯れた枝の上に　しばらくは幻象の重みが持する
また茂る　永遠にくりかえす　無償のみどり
黄色の視線　まれには深紅の微点　ここには
生の乱費　生の惑わし　生の脅威　鳥はとぶ　反映に炎えつ
渇く天の井戸　切実なる死の庇護　夏がすぎて秋へ　蛇はは
いまわる
肉体の到達の場がない　のだろう　寸秒が　滅びが美に値する
異形の卵がふえる　それら雑種の卵が空間をしずかに鎮めて
ゆく
すべてに死のみごもる季節
木の根の瘤　石の下　罌粟の花　落日
あまりにも繁殖する世界　別にもう一つの世界が輝くならば
あまりにも暗い　きのこの密生する地の屋根
雨また雨のふりそそぐ　河のながれ
猛獣はたちまち交尾し　終る　喝采のない田舎芝居の舞台の
　　裡で　叫ぶ
午睡の岩は千丈も裂かれる　神の手も血ぬれて
突然の死と空間の恍惚たる交感状態　夜でも昼でもなく

The Jungle

Trees grow thickly   their fruit ripens   yet withers while the
     foliage is still dense
In the mute silence   outside metaphysics   fruit falls
On the dried branches   the weight of illusion echoes for awhile
Again they grow luxuriantly   eternally repeating the same
     process   greenery gratis
The yellow sight line   on rare occasions a deep red fine point
     here
Life's squandering   life's deception   life's menace   birds fly
     in the reflection, clouds burn continuously
Heaven's well dries up   patron of ardent death   summer passes
     and autumn comes   the snake slithers around
There is no place where corporeality can be attained   a moment's
     squirming   a ruin worthy of beauty
The misshapen eggs increase   and soon the mongrel eggs quietly
     take over the space
For all things, it is a season pregnant with death
A lump on a tree's roots   underneath a stone   a poppy
     the setting sun
A world all too quick to multiply   if another, separate world were
     allowed to shine

皮という皮がむかれて垂れさがる風景
その間からのぞく　青々とした遠方
他になにものも示されない　見えぬ
わずかな極地の薄明に　泛かぶ　結晶する牙　生れながらの
　未だ浄らかな牙の他は

It would be a dark one, so dark   the roof of the earth where
     toadstools grow thickly
Rain and more rain pours down   feeding the river's current
Wild animals quickly copulate   and then it's all over   on the
     stage of an amateurish play for which there is no applause
     naked   they call
The rock used for afternoon naps is covered with thousands of tiny
     cracks   even the hand of God is covered with blood
Sudden death and the ecstatic sympathy of space   there is neither
     day nor night
A landscape in which one after another skins are peeled and hung
     out, dangling
The deep blue distance peering from between the slices of skin
Nothing else to point to   nothing else can be seen
In the twilight of the polar region   they float   crystalized fangs
     their birthright
Purified fangs and nothing more

犬の肖像

1
或る時わたしは帰ってくるだろう
やせて雨にぬれた犬をつれて
他の人にもしその犬の烈しい存在
深い精神が見えなかったらしい
その犬の口をのぞけ
狂気の歯と凍る涎の輝く

2
多くのもの
犬にとっては不用のもの
一人の男にとっては少ないが
意味のあるもの
雑多なところまく缶の灰色
机の上の乾酪
釘くさるズボンのねじれた束
自瀆と枯れた花にわずかに慰められる
破廉恥な生活のわたしの天体
輝く涎の犬は見上げるころがる

Portrait of a Dog

1
At some point I will likely return home
Bringing with me a skinny, rain-soaked dog
If others cannot see the dog's fervent existence
The very depth of his soul
I will tell them to look in his mouth
How the madness of his teeth and the frozen saliva shine

2
Most things
Are unnecessary for a dog
It's not much for a man
But things that are meaningful
Like the ashen color of empty cans scattered about
And the assorted balls of string
Or the cheese left on the desk
And the crumpled pants hanging from a nail
Masturbation and dried flowers
Provide some small measure of comfort
The sphere of my shameless life
The dog with its shining saliva looks up

3
いまわたしのまなびたいことは
木枯の電柱の暗い下で
股の周辺を汚物でぬらしながら
怒りに吠える
匿名の犬の位置へ至ること

4
きわめて自然な路傍の受胎にはじまり
潰れて輝かしい自己の発生に負目なく
しかも一匹の係類にもみとられず
空樽のかたわらで
孤独の骨の存在を終る
雨ざらしの犬

5
たとえば結晶する月の全面く血の爪をかけるほどの
わたしに肉の渇き
心のわたしの飢えが一度でもあったか
わたしの頭をぬらし
わたしの塩辛い眼をながれる
否 雨と真実の汁があったか
わたしは永遠にぬれざる亡霊

6
わたしは犬の鼻をなめねばならぬ
あたらしい生涯の堕落を試みねばならぬ
おびただしい犬の排泄のなかで

7
その犬の舌から全世界の飢えが呼ばれる
その犬の耳から全世界の雨がたれる

3

What I would like to learn now is how
To attain the position of an anonymous dog
How to howl with rage
Under the dark telephone poles in the winter wind
Wetting the area around my thighs with my own filth

4

Conceived by the roadside in the most natural way
Owing nothing for the creation of his defiled, glorious self
Unacknowledged by his own kind
He ends his solitary existence of bones
By the side of an empty barrel
The weather-beaten old dog

5

Was my heart so starved even once
Or flesh so parched I would
Scratch the face of the crystallized moon with bloodied fingernails
Did I ever have the rain and the sweat of truth
Drenching my head
Flowing from my salty eyes
Nay—I am a ghost who doesn't get wet for eternity

6

I must lick the dog's nose
I must try out this new life of depravity
In the prodigal excretion of a dog

7

The hunger of the entire world calls from the dog's tongue
And from his ears drips the rain of the entire world

Born in Laos in 1943, Tuệ Sỹ became a monk at a very early age. In addition to his poetry, he has published books on Zen Buddhism, Buddhist philosophy, and the Chinese poet Du Fu. A well-known dissident in Vietnam, he remains one of the foremost scholars of Buddhism in the country.

Kết Từ

Ngược xuôi nhớ nửa cung đàn
Ai đem quán trọ mà ngăn nẻo về

Last Words

Back and forth, remembering only half the music—
Who put the inn there, blocking the way home?

Contributors

Kareem James Abu-Zeid has lived an itinerant life across the Middle East, Europe, and the U.S. He is an award-winning translator of novels and books of poetry from throughout the Arab world, and also works as a freelance editor and translator of French and German texts into English. He practices various forms of meditation and is currently completing his PhD in comparative literature at UC Berkeley.

Nguyen Ba Chung is a writer, poet, and translator. He is the co-translator of *Thoi Xa Vang* (A Time Far Past); *Mountain River: Vietnamese Poetry from the Wars, 1948–1993*; *Distant Road: Selected Poems of Nguyen Duy*; *Six Vietnamese Poets*; *Zen Poems from Early Vietnam*; and others. He's currently a research associate at the William Joiner Institute at the University of Massachusetts in Boston.

Olivia Baes holds a bachelor's degree in comparative literature and a master's degree in cultural translation from the American University of Paris. For her MA thesis, she translated Swiss author Charles-Ferdinand Ramuz's 1908 novel *Jean-Luc persécuté*. She is currently co-translating a hitherto untranslated work of Marguerite Duras entitled *L'Été 80* with literary translator Emma Ramadan. Olivia is also working on her first novel.

Martha Collins's eighth book of poems, *Admit One: An American Scrapbook*, will be published in 2016 by the University of Pittsburgh. She has also published three volumes of co-translated Vietnamese poetry, most recently *Black Stars: Poems by Ngo Tu Lap* (Milkweed Editions, 2013). She is editor-at-large for *FIELD* magazine and an editor of the Oberlin College Press.

Karen Emmerich is a translator of (modern) Greek literature and Assistant Professor of Comparative Literature at Princeton University. Her recent translations include *The Scapegoat* by Sophia Nikolaidou, *Why I Killed My Best Friend* by Amanda Michalopoulou, and *Diaries of Exile* by Yannis Ritsos, co-translated with Edmund Keeley and winner of the 2014 PEN Poetry in Translation award.

Anne O. Fisher has translated Ilf and Petrov's two novels *The Little Golden Calf* (Russian Life, 2009) and *The Twelve Chairs* (Northwestern University Press, 2011). She lives in Portland, Oregon, with her husband Derek Mong, poet and co-translator of Maxim Amelin's work.

Sibelan Forrester has published translations of poetry, prose, and scholarly works from Croatian, Russian, and Serbian. Recent translations include *The Russian Folktale* by Vladimir Yakovlevich Propp (Wayne State University Press, 2012) and selections of poetry by Maria Stepanova (in *Relocations*, Zephyr Press, 2013). She is coeditor with Martha Kelly of *Russian Silver Age Poetry: Texts and Contexts* (Academic Studies Press, 2015). She teaches Russian language and literature at Swarthmore College in Pennsylvania.

Deborah Iwabuchi, a long-time resident of Japan and raised in the San Francisco Bay Area, has been translating novels, memoirs, and marketing research for over twenty-five years. The novel *Translucent Tree* by Nobuko Takagi (Vertical, 2008) is her favorite work to date. Others include translations of novels by best-selling Japanese authors

Miyuki Miyabe and Jun'ichi Watanabe. Deborah works out of her Southern Exposure Translations office in Maebashi, a beautiful town just far enough away from Tokyo.

Margaret Jull Costa has been a literary translator for nearly thirty years and has translated works by such writers as Eça de Queirós, José Saramago, and Javier Marías. She has won various prizes, most recently the Marsh Award for Children's Literature in Translation for Bernardo Atxaga's *The Adventures of Shola*.

J. Kates is a literary translator who lives in Fitzwilliam, New Hampshire.

David Keplinger is the author of four volumes of poetry, most recently *The Most Natural Thing* (2013) and *The Prayers of Others* (2006). He has won the T. S. Eliot Prize for Poetry (1999), the C. P. Cavafy Poetry Prize (2013), the Erskine J. Poetry Prize (2005), the Colorado Book Award (2007), a fellowship from the National Endowment for the Arts, and other honors. He teaches at American University in Washington, DC.

Derek Mong is the author of two poetry collections from Saturnalia Books, *Other Romes* (2011) and *The Identity Thief* (forthcoming in 2018). His translations (with co-translator Anne O. Fisher) have appeared in *Lunch Ticket*, *Asymptote*, *The Brooklyn Rail*, and elsewhere. Their interview with Maxim Amelin is available online at *Jacket2*.

Jerome Rothenberg is an internationally celebrated poet, translator, and performer with over ninety books of poetry and twelve assemblages of traditional and avant-garde poetry such as *Technicians of the Sacred and Poems for the Millennium*, Volumes 1–3. His most recent books are *Eye of Witness: A Jerome Rothenberg Reader* and

Barbaric Vast & Wild (*Poems for the Millennium*, Volume 5), both published by Black Widow Press.

Eric Selland is a the author of *Arc Tangent* (Isobar Press, 2013). His translation of *The Guest Cat*, a novel by Takashi Hiraide, was on the New York Times Best Seller list in February 2014. Eric currently lives in Tokyo where he works as a translator of economic reports.

Sholeh Wolpé is a poet, editor, and literary translator. A recipient of the 2014 PEN/Heim Translation Fund Award, 2013 Midwest Book Award, and 2010 Lois Roth Persian Translation Prize, Sholeh is the author of three collections of poetry and three books of translations, and is the editor of three anthologies. Her latest book, a modern translation of *Conference of the Birds* by Attar, the twelfth-century Iranian mystic poet, will be released by W. W. Norton in 2017.

Jeffrey Yang is the author of the poetry books *Vanishing-Line* and *An Aquarium*. He is the translator of Su Shi's *East Slope*, Liu Xiaobo's *June Fourth Elegies*, and co-translator of Ahmatjan Osman's *Uyghurland: The Farthest Exile*. He has edited two poetry anthologies for New Directions Publishing: *Birds, Beasts, and Seas* and *Time of Grief*. His translation of Bei Dao's autobiography, *City Gate, Open Up*, is forthcoming from New Directions.

Credits

Amelin, Maxim. "Klassicheskaya oda V. V. Mayakovskomu" and "Zver' ognedyshashchiy s pyshnoyu grivoy…" in *Gnutaya rech'*. Moscow: B.S.G. Press, 2011.

Fraile, Medardo. "En vilo." In *Cuentos de verdad*. Madrid: Ediciones Cátedra, 1964. "Treading Lightly" printed with permission from Andrea Fraile. All rights reserved.

Grekova, I. Excerpt from *Svezho predanie*. Moscow: Text Publishers, 2008.

Huerta, Efraín. Poems from *Poemínimos completos*. Mexico City: Verdehalago, 1999.

Ikonomou, Christos. "Kati tha ginei, tha deis." In *Kati tha ginei, tha deis*. Athens: Polis, 2010. "Something Will Happen, You'll See" printed with permission from Archipelago Books. All rights reserved.

Jaber, Rabee. Excerpt from *al-i'tirafat*. Beirut: dar al-adab li- nashr wa-tawzi', 2008. Excerpt from *Confessions* printed with permission from New Directions Publishing Corp. All rights reserved.

Ramuz, Charles-Ferdinand. Excerpt from *Jean-Luc persécuté*. Paris: Editions Bernard Grasset, 1930.

Takagi, Nobuko. "Tomosui." In *Tomosui*. Tokyo: Shinchosha, 2011.

Tazhi, Aigerim. "Volynistye belye linii..." and "Zapolniaia raspisaniie ostavsheisia zhizni..." in *Bog-o-Slov*. N.p.: Almaty, 2003. "Na ladan ne dyshi—dyshat' zdes' nechem..." and "veter v komnate. dozhd'..." previously unpublished.

Tuệ Sỹ. "Kết Từ." In *Giấc Mơ Trường Sơn*. N.p.: An Tiêm, 2002.

Wagner, Jan. "koi" and "pieter codde: bildnis eines mannes mit uhr." In *Regentonnenvariationen*. Berlin: Hanser Berlin Verlag, 2014. "rübezahl." In *Australien*. Berlin: Berlin Verlag, 2010. "klatschmohn." Previously unpublished.

Yang, Jeffrey. "And Thirst." Previously unpublished. Figure 1 reprinted from Richard E. Strassberg, *A Chinese Bestiary: Strange Creatures from the Guideways through Mountains and Seas* (Berkeley: University of California Press, 2002). Figures 2–6 reprinted from 马昌仪 Ma Changyi, ed. 古本山海經圖說 *Gu ben shan hai jing tu shuo* (Guilin, China: Guangxi Normal University Press, 2009: 2 volumes, revised and expanded edition).

Yoshioka, Minoru. "Guuwa," "Janguru," and "Inu no Shouzou." In *Seibutsu in Yoshioka Minoru Zenshishuu*. Tokyo: Chikuma Shobo, 1996.

Zarrinpour, Behzad. "Taboot-hayeh bi daro-paykar" ("Lidless Coffins with No Bodies"). Previously unpublished.

Index by Language